On the Shores of Lake Onyx

and other weird tales

Ayd Instone

Reviews of 'A Voice in the Light':

Stories to challenge and inspire the mind
"If you're looking for short stories that will not only challenge your mind whilst you read them, but also inspire you to pick up a pen and start writing your own, then this book is definitely for you. Perhaps best described as a cross between the science fiction of The Twilight Zone, mixed with the delightfully odd Britishness of Tales of the Unexpected, there should be something for everyone in this collection. Whether it's the lonely tale of a lighthouse in deep space, the disturbing case of an artificial intelligence in the frame for murder, or what really caused the Sumarian empire to crumble, each story leaves you thinking in a way that all good fiction should. At this price, for storytelling with such imagination, you really can't afford not to pick up this book."

– J Mahon

A really good humored (in every sense of the word) and intelligent read.
"I found a copy of this in the bookshelves of a library. This is really pleasant science fiction, low on nasty, pointless violence and gore, with carefully thought out and intriguing stories - it's certainly suitable for young adult readers. This is a book you can dip in and out of and it becomes obvious, the more stories you read, that the author genuinely is a scientist himself. A really good humored (in every sense of the word) and intelligent read."

– S. H. Clark

A twist in the tail
"From the first story I was delighted with the clever twists and turns that took something that sounded recognisable and suddenly it was not what it seemed to be. It's a great book to read when you have a few spare moments and want to stretch your mind until it escapes from the 'box'. Ayd Instone's passion for imagination and taking the ordinary into the extraordinary is in every story."

– Lesley Morrissey

Unique
Totally weird! Great to read something original. Loads of succinct short stories with catchy plots and intriguing themes. Great value too."

– Chris Michael

Short but powerful stories

"He presents brilliant, powerful, believable ideas in small packages. They may be short, but the concepts presented are wonderfully original and many left me reeling from being smacked around the cerebral cortex. Ayd may not write in prose (yet) but his works bring to mind Roald Dahl's short stories, the ideas of Jorge Luis Borges, and classic British horror like Alan Garner. Stories which are so rooted in reality that when they splinter away from what we know, the effect is far deeper and more believable than far fetched science fiction writings where the reader is often required to believe in and support a massive construct of science fantasy. It's my belief that anyone can learn to write, but having great ideas is a rarer gift. I believe Ayd could take his ideas to great places and personally hope he does so."

– John Bloor

Twilight Zone fans will love this! I read it several times

"This collection is very provocative, stretching the imagination in truly untraditional ways. Often, at the end of the story, there will be one last twist that actually makes me gasp with surprised delight. Some of the tales are pure sci-fi, some are pure ghost story - and some combine the two, which is really fun. All of them will make you think. Excellent illustrations, too. They are as bold and mysterious as the tales themselves. Those zinger endings are brilliant every single time. Some of them make me cry for joy, some make me shiver with fear, and some just leave my jaw hanging. Instone has really thought about things in some mind-stretchy ways, and none of these stories feels like a parrot of some other work. The very fact that I've read the stories now three or four times each shows that I can find something new to appreciate each time through."

– Mrs G.

Thought Provoking

"This collection of short stories is a gem; brimming with imaginative ideas and written so well that it is a shame when you get to the end of each, but easy to go back and read all over again. The endings are never what you think they are going to be which adds to the intrigue. Highly recommended."

– Michael Rocharde

SUNMAKERS

Text ©2018 Ayd Instone

On the Shores of Lake Onyx and other weird tales

Published by Sunmakers
www.sunmakers.co.uk

Version 1.0

Designed and illustrated by Ayd Instone.
Author photo by Haddon Davies, www.haddondavies.com
Cover image Pavel Parmenov www.123rf.com
References for 'A Voice in the Dark': http://www.dailymail.co.uk/home/moslive/article-1348690/Dark-matter-A-British-led-Yorkshire-try-solve-universes-biggest-mystery.html.
J. Delingpole, 2011.
'Magic Mirror' illustration inspired by artwork by Clive, Terminal Software, 1983

The right of Ayd Instone to be identified as the author of this work has been asserted by him in accordance with the Copyright, Designs and Patents Act, 1988

No part of this publication may be reproduced, hosted or transmitted by any means without the publisher's written permission.

ISBN: 978-1-908693-25-9

www.aydinstone.com

To Chris. Thanks for the 25 years of big nights out.

Also by
Ayd Instone

The Voice in the Light
and other weird tales.

Don't Tell the Dinosaurs
(The Secrets of the Future)

Ding!
How to Have a Great Idea

7 Keys to Creative Genius

Contents

Luminous Awe: an introduction 11

On the Shores of Lake Onyx 19
A mission to Saturn's moon, Titan, finds something wholly unexpected.

The Keeper at Hobs' Point 31
A young man finds himself doubting the skepticism of old maritime superstitions as mythological sea creatures around a mysterious Whitby lighthouse close in.

The Queen of Cups 43
A group of survey archeologists in the future use technology to explore an environment in more than just three dimensions. They find evidence of genocide, but whose history are they seeing and are they equipped to handle the consequences?

Magic Mirror 59
Can an ancient mirror really foretell the fate of those reflected in it?

The Moth 73
Could something as simple as a fluttering insect drive you insane?

Secret of the Circle 77
Himmler's final despicable experiments are discovered on a remote island.

The Fly 97
Everyone has their price. What are you prepared to sell to
gain success?

The Glasshouse 103
A new teacher in a remote boarding school becomes embroiled in
an ancient mystery surrounding a strange glass structure.

Council of Hex................................... 119
What would you do with an artefact that could bend others to your
will?

The Shadow People............................. 129
Told as a thread on Facebook. A cautionary tale about things that
lurk in the corner of your eye as the users of internet devices
discover the frightening downside of too much screen-time.

Crystals of Consciousness....................... 141
A rescue mission turns into something that makes a man question
his entire existence.

Silver Light 159
Traditional photography with an antique camera allows unusual
light to produce ghostly results.

Two Heads....................................... 169
An ingenious new method of artificial intelligence is more
successful than expected.

The Curse of Baphomet 189
Could research into devil worship, the manna machine and
masonic treasure unearth the source of all evil?

Ghosts 213
What is the nature of ghosts? Do they really exist?

Night School 221
A teacher encounters an uninvited student appearing in class after
hours demanding to be taught.

The Ghost of Tracey Pemberton 229
In a small village with its prejudices, bigotry and casual violence,
what could be behind the disappearance of a young girl?

The Voice in the Dark 251
What if darkness isn't just the absence of light, but something in its
own right? Set in and around the Whitby countryside.

About the Author 226

On the Shores of Lake Onyx and other weird tales

Luminous Awe: an Introduction

'Suppose you were told there was a tiger in the next room: you would know that you were in danger and would probably feel fear,'[1] thus spake C.S. Lewis in his exploration of the numinous. In that statement Lewis describes everything that is wrong with many modern ghost stories and especially big budget horror films and those that feature the supernatural: they are reduced to a clear understandable fear of death or injury, whether it be from a tiger, a madman with an axe or even a demonic beast. This type of fear is too predictable and dull.

'But if you were told that there is a ghost in the next room and believed it, you would feel, indeed, what is often called fear, but of a different kind,' continues Lewis. 'It would not be based on the knowledge of danger, for no one is primarily afraid of what a ghost may do to him, but of the mere fact that it is a ghost. It is 'uncanny' rather than dangerous, and the special kind of fear it excites may be called Dread. With the Uncanny one has reached the fringes of the Numinous.'

The word 'numinous' is an English adjective, derived in the 17th century from the Latin 'numen', within Roman paganism, meaning 'a deity or spirit presiding over a thing or space'. The word was popularised by Rudolf Otto in his 1917 book *Das Heilige* (which appeared in English as *The Idea of the Holy* in 1923)[2]. Otto described it as having three parts, 'Mysterium tremendum et fascinans' meaning fearful and fascinating mystery. Mysterium is wholly other. Tremendum signifies awfulness, terror, demonic dread, awe, absolute unapproachability, the sense of one's own nothingness in contrast to an objective presence. Fascinans indicates a potent charm, an attractiveness in spite of fear and terror. The numinous is beyond good and evil, a spiritual realm devoid of morality.

Lewis took it one step further, 'Now suppose that you were told simply, 'There is a mighty spirit in the room,' and believed it. Your feelings would then be even less like the mere fear of danger: but the disturbance would be profound. You would feel wonder and a certain shrinking—a sense of inadequacy to cope with such a visitant of prostration before it... This feeling may be described as awe, and the object which excites it as the Numinous.

With these stories I am not expecting to reach the divine, that is too lofty a goal. It is the purpose of this book to present stories that invoke the state of fear and the numinous, settling just below it. I have called this state of awe 'The Luminous' to encompass the purpose and scope of the stories. The word luminous encapsulates the emitting of light, a shining in the dark, illumination, a high degree of saturation as well as something being perceived clearly or vividly, enlightened or intelligent. That's not entirely the whole truth, the real reason for the use of the luminous is that it was a slip of the tongue when I was trying to explain the 'numinous' to my friend Chris as the theme for our first annual ghost story for Christmas evening. The error seemed to have created something interesting, so it stuck. My goal here is to invite the reader to step right out on the precipice and invoke within them a sense of apeirophobia, that is 'a fear of infinity', what Otto described in Latin as mysterium tremendum, a terrible dread of some wholly overwhelming, almost cyclopean power.

You should find this *Luminous Awe*, as a subset of Horror, to be less about simply fear of death or pain and more about fear of fear itself, of the unknown and unknowable: a fear for your soul (even if you don't know what that is). A good ghost story should make us all shudder. A belief in ghosts is not required, a belief in possibilities is. When horror meets science fiction we have the best of both breeds: a realistic, plausible scenario and chain of events along with a compelling sense of dread. H.P. Lovecraft described his writing process as first working out what emotion he wanted to convey, then he would work out how it was to be conveyed, by what situations, plot and characters, and then by what order would he reveal those ingredients to construct the story (which is exactly that - the manner and order the plot is revealed to the reader). Probably five of the stories in my first book could be described as 'ghost stories' and possibly ten you could call 'science fiction'. It's flipped the other way this time. Probably around ten in this collection may be ghost stories, the rest science fiction.

I've attempted to be as varied and original as possible in addition to getting as many facts correct as I can. In *Secret of the Circle* the facts are closer to the truth than you think, many of the elements featured did exist. Even the mythical elixir of life, 'vril' found its way into the drink Bovril, as in bovine elixir. The myths detailed in *The Curse of Baphomet* are as accurate as I could make them, drawn from various myths and legends. *The Ghost of Tracey Pemberton,* the last to be written for this collection, may or may not even be a ghost story, you can decide.

Part of the motivation to write ghost stories may come from the dissatisfaction I have with the supernatural, that I have researched it enough to see all examples of it vanish. This angle is explored in the story here called simply *Ghosts*. The challenge has been to create a new plausibility to the ghost or an invocation of the uncanny that is as convincing as it is unnerving. Simply using the cliches or stereotypical motifs of ghosts and their standard explanations is not interesting to me. *Magic Mirror* is a pure tale unashamedly in the style of M.R. James whereas *The Keeper at Hobs' Point* attempts to subvert the form by giving a reason, (an explanation being the tenant of science fiction), if not a fantastical reason, to the spooky goings on.

Readers of my first collection will recall the main character of *Black Light*. She proved popular with enough people to warrant a return in both *Two Heads* and *The Voice in the Dark* where her position as the rational scientist is valuable in investigating the strange phenomenon. She even gets a surname in these new stories.

During writing I became self indulgent enough to wonder if there were reoccurring themes in my work. The word luminous seems appropriate as I noticed a preoccupation with the concept of light. My rock band was called Luma Chroma which means light, shade and colour (prior to that we were also called, albeit briefly, Ultra Violet Kipper). The first self-released albums of my songs in 1990/91 were entitled *Magic Lantern* and *Kaleidoscope*. Most of my stories are about, or concern light. In my first book, The *Voice in the Light*, *New Age of Darkness*, *The Lighthouse Keeper*, *Black Light*, *The Magic Candle* and *Stars* dealt with light in some form. In this collection it's true of *Magic Mirror*, *The Glasshouse*, *The Shadow People*, *Silver Light* and *The Voice in the Dark* and the lighthouse figures in *The Keeper at Hobs' Point*.

In popular music they call it 'the difficult second album' - you've used up all your best songs on your debut which effectually you've been working on all your life up to that point and then... a second instalment is needed in hardly any time at all. The cupboard is bare of ideas, the barrel has been scrapped. Where is the new material going to come from? It's a real test of your creativity and staying power. Is it the same with a short story collection? Ironically I have enough songs written for my first fifty albums, but short stories - I'd put the latest and best plus some scrapped from long past, reaching back to my youth in that first volume, *A Voice in the Light*. There were all there, those eighteen tales, there were no more. The stories that didn't make that first collection didn't make it for a reason so they were out. So all these stories are brand new? Not quite. On exploring the attic looking for my old school exercise books, I came across a couple of sheets of handwritten file paper with a story I'd forgotten all about that a twenty year old me had written (*The Moth*) and another that I'd written as a screenplay with the intention of filming as a short film (*The Fly*), originally entitled *A Speck of Dust*. So there are those two older stories presented here, but all the rest are new since the first collection. That means I have entered into that strange experience of the state of 'not having an idea' and then entering into 'having an idea' sixteen times within these pages. I'd be sitting somewhere wishing I had an idea for a story. Then, sometime soon afterwards I'd have that idea. Where did it come from? When I've written a story there's a brief glow of excitement and pride, like waking up on Christmas morning and opening a gift of an exquisite multifaceted crystal and I stare into its brilliance for hours. Then, after a day or so, it loses its lustre and becomes dull. I feel low and worthless, dejected and bored. The only cure is to write another. Then the hunt is on again, the excitement of the chase resumes, and the cycle continues.

I remember seeing an interview with Alan Bennett just prior to the broadcast of his second series of *Talking Heads* monologues in the late 1980s. "They're sadder than the first lot," he said. I feel similarly about this collection in that it's darker than the first one. But I like them more. I think they're better. Without darkness, you can't appreciate the light, so we need this dark to contrast this 'luminous' I've attempted to invoke.

Ayd Instone
Whitby
November 2017

---

[1] Lewis, C.S. (1940). *The Problem of Pain*, William Collins
[2] Otto, R. (1923). *The Idea of the Holy* (Trans. John W. Harvey.) Oxford: Oxford University Press, 1923; 2nd ed.

On the Shores of Lake Onyx and other weird tales

On the Shores of Lake Onyx

On the Shores of Lake Onyx and other weird tales

On the Shores of Lake Onyx

I set out early that day, hoping to see another Saturn rise. The haze looked thinner that morning as I'd hoped, more mustard brown rather than the usual burnt orange of methane and ethane clouds in the nitrogen-rich organic smog. Even though the cliff was about a kilometre away I could get there easily with the low gravity, it's quite a relaxing walk. I've never been on the Moon, but I think I'd prefer Titan anyway, the Moon is just too bleak, white, unchanging and, let's face it, a bit dull. At least on Titan, you feel you're getting somewhere with your bounces, kicking up the dark sooty ice sand. Sometimes in the night the wind has created more ripples and dunes. Most days there's a rainfall of various organic compounds, created in the upper atmosphere by the ultraviolet radiation of the Sun. The rainfall washes down the ice hills as dark rivers flowing down to the black lakes. Sometimes the polymer ice sand has been blown away to reveal interesting rock formations. But it's the view down over the lakes I like the most.

We'd been on Titan for six months now, working quite hard enlarging Base One. With the Forge fully operational we were making great progress, way ahead of schedule. So we could afford more days off until the next supply arrived, probably within two weeks, it having just left Jupiter. Abdalla had his poetry, Roshami her paintings, I just had my thoughts. I'd make it to the cliff edge and looked out over the methane lake, looking up at the majesty of old father Saturn and those rings. As you know, we go around every fifteen days and twenty-two hours, locked in a synchronous rotation, always showing the same face to the planet. But you don't always get to see it, it entirely depends on the weather. That day, there was little wind and as I've said, the haze was thinner than usual. It never really gets very bright. It's always dusk, always gloomy, with about a hundredth of the brightness you get on Earth. I got right up to the cliff edge and looked over. There, about five hundred meters or so down, was Lake Onyx.

In the suit you're not aware how cold it is out there. It all looks normal and Earth like in a way, except at -173°C, it's not water you're looking at but liquid methane. You know all about the life forms we found. People got used to the idea so quickly they lost that sense of wonder. It still amazes me that the life that evolved here has no link to life on Earth. I think when ordinary people learnt that the alien life forms were simple multicellular and mainly microscopic they lost interest. There can be nothing we would call plant life as plants need sunlight as their energy source to photosynthesise. The creatures we found are not really animals either, having their own unique chemistry. They're a whole new kingdom altogether, but most similar to fungi. The ones we've studied inhale hydrogen instead of oxygen and metabolise it with acetylene instead of glucose, exhaling methane instead of carbon dioxide.

It was because of the good weather, and spurred on by the fantastic view of Saturn, that I decided today would be a good day to climb down the cliff to the lake. I relayed a few images back to base. I knew my location was being constantly monitored by the systems at the base and anyway, taking calculated risks was what we were all about. Otherwise we wouldn't be here in the first place.

I took care climbing down. Not because it was difficult, but because it was all too easy and I had to be sure with each step that I could get back up. It took less than twenty minutes to descend and another thirty to get close to the edge of the lake. I hadn't noticed in my concentration that I had descended into a deeper, darker gloom. Clouds must have moved in. Looking up I could no longer see Saturn clearly. Oddly, looking across the lake now, I was no longer moved by its beauty but instead felt an odd feeling of foreboding and shivered looking across its black unreflective surface. The liquid lapped at the shore near my feet. Within the suit I could not hear the sound of it splashing over the dark ice pebbles that lined the shore, but presumably it did make a sound. I picked up one of the larger pebbles (all I could manage with my gauntleted hand) and threw it as far as I could into the lake. It created a silent black splash. Dark ripples circled out for a few seconds and then nothing. The lake returned to it's featureless state. I bent down to pick up another pebble and there, under the rock was what looked like a dark black slug or leech. As I looked, it slithered over the rock. I flung it immediately into the lake in disgust, then cursed my reflex for losing what should have been a great discovery: a macro life-form on this moon, large enough to see with the naked eye. Realising my mistake I frantically lifted pebble after pebble in a vain hope to discover another specimen. I needn't have worried. Bending down I saw around a dozen of them had clambered onto my boots. At least I wouldn't have to think of a way to carry one back, I'd simply walk back with these passengers and outside the base scape them off and get a cryo-tube to take a few inside. I turned to retrace my steps back to the cliff. But that wasn't as easy as I'd expected. I'd walked the distance in around half an hour, probably under a kilometre and from the cliff I could see the lake easily. Looking back, the gloom had increased to such a degree that I couldn't even make out the cliff. All I knew was that it must lie in the opposite direction to the lake. But ahead was just blackness. I set off anyway. The gloom gave just enough light for me to be able to see where I was putting my feet, but no more. I turned on my chest mounted torch, but in the thick smog it made progress more difficult, giving out a short column of light that lit up nothing. I turned it off. After around forty minutes I became a little anxious. I should have reached the incline by now. The surface underfoot had changed, from the loose pebbles to a more solid rocky sharpness. After a few more minutes I came upon chest height rocks that I haven't come across on the way out. I guessed I must have traveled a bit too far to the left or right, but that the cliff must still lay ahead. Clambering over the large rocks I could see a darker patch ahead in the dark. I must have met the cliff except from this side the gentle gradient I had climbed down was not there, instead a shear face met me. I was not over concerned as all I would need to do would be to follow this cliff face until such a point it became climbable. But the cliff presented not a clear topography. It curved inwards into what I imagined was a bay. I had no choice but to stick to the cliff wherever it should lead. After another fifteen minutes of walking the cliff face opened up into some sort of cave. Sensing this was worth turning my torch on again for, I shone the light into it. The ice walls sparkled. This was worth investigating, I radioed the base to report my position and intent before entering. Oddly, I heard nothing but static. I'd been out for just over an hour so a brief look would be fine before returning to climb the cliff and to hopefully get a signal.

After just a few metres into the crystal cave it appeared I'd reached the far wall but instead the cave floor ramped downwards in a manner that coincidentally and conveniently resembled a wide stone stairway. Going down a stairway in low gravity is all too easy. It more or less went straight down, widening out as it did so. I had descended roughy the height of two or three floors and at the bottom I found myself in a large circular grotto. The fact that the cavern, the stairway and this cave must have been carved out by natural erosion, I hadn't questioned, until I swung around to shine my light around the room.

Around the edges were giant, perfectly carved archways, each three meters high, presumably leading onto other chambers. There were seven of them. But the strangest and most shocking of all was

On the Shores of Lake Onyx and other weird tales

what stood in the centre of the grotto. On a plinth sat a metre diameter perfectly polished sphere. It was a model of Saturn, complete with rings, made from translucent coloured ice rock. This was a shock to my system. Explorers had only arrived on Titan a decade ago, and not in this locale until us, and yet another mission had clearly been here before us. The workmanship on the model was exquisite. The rings were so delicately formed, only a few millimetres thick. I recorded it all, unable to relay the images back of course.

Then it happened. I reached out my hand to touch the globe. As I did so there was a tiny spark of static that made me jump back. The entire model of Saturn lit up, illuminated by some light source in the plinth. Behind and all around me, dull red glows came from each of the seven archways. My suit had no external microphone to hear any sounds, but through my boots I could feel a regular pulsating rhythm. There was sound in this place. I walked slowly over to one of the red archways. They were shallow alcoves and inside another surprise awaited me. Standing, or sitting, I couldn't tell which, was some kind of giant three metre tall creature, perfectly still. Its surface was shiny and black, like the leeches on my boots earlier. At first it was hard to make out its form, there were so many protuberances. On closer inspection I could make out a spindly central body with three longer jointed limbs pointing downwards, presumably legs, and seven tentacle like limbs coming from the central torso. The other protuberances were attached to the walls of the alcove and made me think they were tubes connecting the creature to something that perhaps had once sustained it in its hibernation or preserved it in its death. At the top of the body was a triangular shape that could be referred to as a head. Three large circles, arranged in an upside down triangle formation, were the only visible feature. Could they be eyes? The overall appearance gave me not a sense of wonder, but one of fear and dread. This thing, was it alive? Had it ever been alive? How long had it been here? I backed away from the alcove and examined the others briefly. They too had a thing sat inside. All except one that is. One was empty, the tubes from the walls hung limp. I had the overwhelming urge to exit the cavern, but in the low gravity I turned too quickly. The floor was too smooth and in my haste to run, I slipped and slid towards the model of Saturn. I reached out my arms to stop my fall, my elbows colliding with the delicate rings. They shattered as I fell forward, a shard of glassy polymer ice pierced my suit near my right shoulder. I knew I must get in radio contact immediately and bounded for the stairway with as much speed as I could. I could feel the pressure of the thick atmosphere blowing into the gash on my suit as I reached the upper cave and struggled outside to the cliff. The freezing cold nitrogen had destroyed my shoulder at that point and my right arm hung uselessly. The deep freeze spread down my right side as I raced away from the cliff to hope for a signal. It worked and I sent my emergency distress message, just as the freeze destroyed my chest and I fell forwards to the shingled ground. The deadly freeze solidified me up to my neck and then I remembered no more.

'We'll keep you on file until the shipment arrives. It should be possible to do repairs, but until then we don't have enough parts to do a proper job,' said Andrez after I'd finished my account. 'There's still coordination work you can do until we get you a new body.'

'The images you captured are intriguing,' said Roshami, flicking through my recordings on the screen. 'We'll relay them back to Earth and see what further instructions we receive.'

'What happened to my body?' I asked.

'Frozen solid,' said Abdalla, 'and now recycled. We downloaded you just in time.'

'And what of the creatures? Do we think they are or were alive?' I asked.

'We picked you up not knowing about the cave until now so we have made no further investigation as yet,' said Andrez. 'The fact that we now find macro life forms and some evidence of intelligence and design is fascinating.'

The next day Roshami and Abdalla returned together to the cavern. We discussed their findings upon their return a few hours later.

'The lighting was off as we entered, just as it had been for you,' said Abdalla. 'Touching the globe still worked as you had reported, even with the broken rings. We studied the creatures in the alcoves. All six were identical. There was no sign of the missing seventh.'

'We do not know for what reason they were in hibernation, but we do know they had been there over twenty thousand years,' added

Roshami.

'Were they alive?' I asked.

'No,' she replied. 'They were like us, synthetic life forms. Perhaps like us, made in the image of their creators, but designed to function on Titan. Perhaps like us, to perform some kind of exploratory mission.'

A short while later the message from Earth came through. We were told that in light of the discoveries, the supply ship had turned around and was retuning to Jupiter. We were to close all but essential systems down and return to our cryo chambers and go offline until further instructions. Earth didn't want anything further disrupted until more decisions could be made on the best way forward. Intelligent life, capable of building automatons and the technology in the cavern had never been found in the Solar System thus far. There would be debates and discussions back on Earth about how to proceed. Everything was put on standby. Roshami, Abdalla, Andrez and the three other members of our team entered their cryo chambers and were deactivated. As I was integrated into the main systems I could operate the partial shutdown easily and put all systems offline. We would now sleep until our masters were ready to awaken us again for us to continue their work.

The Keeper at Hobs' Point

On the Shores of Lake Onyx and other weird tales

The Keeper at Hobs' Point

It was Jack Hargreaves' first proper job. He'd helped his uncle on his fishing boat since he was a young boy and now he was a Trainee Keeper at Hobs' Point. They'd taken the poor lad in after a freak accident claimed the lives of his father and uncle. The lad needed a fresh start to break him out of his melancholy and it was a generous offer. It was the year 1900 and Jack had just turned sixteen. The lighthouse had been built in 1811 on the foundations of its 1608 predecessor. It was fitted with a modern gas lamp that was thirteen times more powerful than the most brilliant light then known, dramatically better than the old greasy whale oil powered lamps the region had been used to. The fact that the lighthouse was haunted was well known and Jack did not have long to wait before his first encounter with something unnatural.

The island was small and the lighthouse was at the highest point making it look even taller than it was. There was a rocky path down to a flatter outcrop where the gas cylinders were housed. The path spiralled down from there to a tiny jetty where the small boat that had brought the three keepers was moored. Other than that, there was just black rock, sharp and jagged, slashed by waves, surrounded by the deep cold water of the North Sea.

There was a fog coming up that night so the men and the boy were on alert. The lamp was lit and the horn was sounded at regular intervals. The main keeper was an old Welshman (they called him Jones the Lamp). Then there was Jim Maidstone and the boy Jack. Jack was on watch at the top of the tower. Leaning over the rails he could see nothing. The air was strangely still with thick fog and with the flashing of the lamp he could see only alternate whiteness and blackness. But there was a sound. It was coming from the rocks below. It was a woman's voice. At that moment old Jones had returned to the top.

'Did you hear that sir? I thought I heard a voice.' said Jack.

'A voice boy? Where?' said Jones.

'A woman's voice sir, from down there,' said the boy.

'Nothing down there boy. Just the rocks,' said Jones. 'You get back below boy, it's cold up here tonight.'

Jack went down the spiral staircase, but didn't stop at the crew room. He went all the way down to the main door and out on the rocks. He heard the woman's voice again. It was clearer this time, coming from the south side of the tiny island. With a lamp in hand, Jack scrambled over the rocks and lowered himself down near the waters edge.

The voice sounded like "Help me, help me" or "Come here, come here".

'Hold on miss,' Jack replied, 'I'm nearly there.'

He put the lamp carefully down on a rock and lowered himself down. Just as he did, someone grabbed his arm. He caught sight of a beautiful woman with long golden hair in a flowing green dress, sat on the rock, before whirling round to meet his assailant. It was Maidstone.

'Quick lad, get back up here,' said Maidstone, pulling Jack back up to the rocks above. Soon they were back on the path and Maidstone pushed the lad back inside the building and up to the crew room.

'But the lady!' protested Jack.

'Give him a drop of brandy. But not too much mind,' said Jones, coming down the stairs, 'there was no lady down there boy.'

'But I saw her!' said Jack.

'Probably a seal,' said Maidstone, 'You saw what you thought you saw in the dark.'

'There's no point Maidstone. Tell him the truth,' said Jones.

'I know I saw a woman, and heard her too,' protested Jack.

'You saw something all right,' said Jones, 'but it was no woman. We've all seen them, every now and then, tempting us out onto the rocks. You're special lad. A new keeper usually has to wait a few months before seeing anything. You're lucky.'

'What are you saying?' said Jack, 'Some kind of, what are they called, sirens?'

'We call 'em the Hobs. You sees what you expects to see, what you wants to see,' said Jones.

'Now you're scaring the lad, Jones,' said Maidstone.

'If he's going to be here, he needs to know,' said Jones.

'Did you see her there just now?' Jack asked Maidstone.

'I saw nothing lad,' he replied.

'Depends what you mean by seeing,' said Jones. 'And I won't ever see what you see.'

We walked along the beach, Jack and I as he told me his story. The old man, now eighty-six, was kicking the thick large seaweed stems that completely covered the sand as we walked along.

'It's black kelp isn't it?' I said

'If you say so,' he said. 'Loosened by the squall, washed up in the storm.'

I'd been telling him a little of what I did.

'Them computers. What if you joined 'em all up, to make one big one, all of them thinking together. Would that be a brain you think?' he said.

'No, a mainframe doesn't need to be connected to anything, it's powerful enough as it is. Perhaps you could have them linked in the future. But I don't know what it would achieve and it won't make a brain as such. Computers are not clever, they're just quicker than us at calculations,' I said.

'If you got lots of 'em, millions or 'em. Each one might not be bright, but together. Each one like a bit of a brain,' he said.

'I see, like loads of brain cells. There aren't that many

computers, and they're quite big. They are getting smaller though. A lot of computing power was needed for the Moon landing last year,' I added. We walked up to the harbour and out along the pier. Jack pointed out to sea beyond the southern headland.

'When the Abbey was built it was three miles inland, not close to the cliff like now. They say the Romans were the first to put a beacon on the end of the peninsular. It was cut off from the mainland for over five hundred years,' Jack said.

I looked out to the empty sea where he was indicating.

'Centuries of erosion have done their job. Our little island was the last remnant of the headland out there and a real hazard to shipping. Perhaps it's just as well.'

The men on the lighthouse did not discuss the events of that night again. It was now a given. Jack knew the others heard voices, or saw something too, but what they made of it, he never knew.

'It's low tide when you're more likely as not to see 'em,' Jones had said. Other than that there was no further mention.

It was late October when the second incident happened. Jack had got up early and walked out on the island, as far as a short stroll and a climb could be called 'a walk', to get the best view of the golden sunrise. It was a particularly low tide which meant the rocks were about eight feet higher above the surface of the sea and a plateau of rocks normally under the water were visible, and accessible. As he looked out to the copper coloured sky and liquid gold water, Jack heard singing. He followed the voice, a woman's voice, down onto the newly revealed rocks. He was cautious as they were completely covered in the giant pale green slimy stalks of kelp. It was all over the base of the rocky island, every surface was wrapped in the stuff. As he lowered himself down, the singing stopped and a voice whispered.

'Trust me, Jack. Trust me.'

This time though, he saw no-one. After waiting around for a short time, and noticing that the tide was slowly coming in, Jack clambered back up to the lighthouse to make breakfast. He didn't say anything to the others.

A month later, Maidstone was ill in bed with some sort of fever. New cylinders had been brought up to supply both the lamp, their lighting and the cooker. Jones and Jack had to manage the installation on their own which was a difficult job with a man down. That evening Jack had taken Maidstone his supper up before joining Jones in the lamp room at the top.

'This mist is getting thicker. The wind is dropping. It looks like becoming a real dense fog,' said Jones, looking out to sea as the last of the sun faded away. 'You go and put the kettle on.'

Jack turned to go down the stairs but a sound stopped him in his tracks.

'Did you hear that Jones?' he said.

'What's that boy?' Jones replied.

'The woman's voice again. Singing. Come on you must hear it!' said Jack.

'Just the wind boy. Now you be careful. It's another low tide tonight. Don't be getting any ideas about what you see or don't see, hear or don't hear! Just get that tea.'

Jack delivered the tea up to Jones. Perhaps the singing had faded, perhaps it was still there. He went back down to the kitchen and there it was again. This time he swore the voice was calling his name.

'Come out, come out. Jack, come out!' he thought he heard.

Slowly Jack crept down and outside. He took a lamp with him. The voice came from the same place as before.

'Come down Jack, come down. Quickly!' it said.

Jack got to the place where he'd been before, standing on the slippery kelp. He shone his light around. Then, just a bit lower down from where he was, just a few feet away, he saw a woman in the shadows. Long golden hair she had and a flowing green dress.

'This way Jack, this way,' she said before disappearing off to the right.

Jack clambered further down and shone his lamp to where the figure was just a moment ago. There, on the underside of an outcrop was a small cave. It was easy to get to. The voice came from within it.

'Come in, Jack, come in.'

Jack went in. The small dank, wet cave, carved by the sea was also filled with the slimy kelp. But there was no lady. At that moment there was a tremendous explosion, a brilliant flash of light and the whole rock shook. Jack rushed out of the cave in shock and was horrified to look up to see the burning remains of the north side of the island. The lighthouse had been totally destroyed.

'It was a gas explosion. They confirmed it later,' Jack said, still looking out to sea from the pier. 'I went back to fishing for a time. The storms that winter broke up what was left of the island. The explosion must have weakened it somehow.'

He changed the subject and asked me why I was here and not at the university. I felt as though it would be okay to reveal the truth but he seemed to somehow know in his next statement.

'It's a funny thing, the mind. Just when you think everything is going well you find yourself not enjoying it as you think you should. You blame yourself for not being happy for no reason and that makes it worse, I know,' he said.

So I didn't need to tell him I was on extended leave, told to go off and relax, find myself, take some time. I didn't want to admit there had been something wrong with me but there was. I could admit that now as these sea walks made it all seem so far away and unimportant.

'They saved me you see,' Jack continued. He turned away from the sea and we started walking back to the beach.

'They?' I asked. 'You mean the woman?'

'There was no woman. That's just how they showed themselves,' Jack said.

'The hobs?'

Jack picked up a stalk from the sand.

'Seaweed is not a plant. It's not an animal. It's something else, some other life. You know that?' he said.

'Some sort of algae isn't it? Biology's not my subject I'm afraid,' I said.

'It's like a sponge, like coral. It's alive. It helped me. That's how I think of it. They worked out a way to speak to me, right into my brain, and when I needed to be helped, they got me into the only safe hiding place. They knew what was going to happen. I don't know if it was Jones and me installing the gas wrong or if the increased pressure blew through a crack in a pipe somewhere. I don't know. But I do know I was saved by them.'

We were on the beach now. The tide was further in and had washed away most of the kelp from before. It was also quite dark and I knew I had to be getting back to my boarding house before my landlady locked up for the night. I said goodbye to the old man and we went our separate ways.

The next day the sun was out. In more ways than one. I set off in a fine mood, the sky was clearer than I could remember in a long, long while. I wanted to meet up with Jack again but he was nowhere to be found. I tried the places he'd mentioned to me in his earlier conversations but no-one knew who I was talking about. I tried the local museum to see if there were any clues to be found there. I approached a woman who was behind a cash desk, dusting the surface between stacks of postcards.

'Do you have any pictures of the old lighthouse?' I asked.

You mean the pier lighthouse?' she said.

'No, on the island, Hobs' Point,' I said.

She looked at me blankly.

'The lighthouse on the island off the headland. The one that blew up around 1900,' I said.

She looked at me strangely.

'Nothing like that around here and I've lived here fifty years. Never heard of anything like that in Whitby. Are you sure it was here, not Saltburn or somewhere?

I paused, puzzled and thought about how I felt and what I'd seen, or thought I'd seen. One postcard caught my eye. It had a painting on it of a woman, a bit like a mermaid, dressed in green, sat on some rocks, combing her golden hair. I bought it and left. Outside, I looked at the postcard again. On the back it said, 'The Kelpie' and next to that a name, 'by Jack Hargreaves.'

Shortly after that I returned to the university, and my work, a new project based on the idea of local area networks, a protocol to allow computers to talk to one another, to create a sort of interwoven network. I still have the postcard. I often look at it and wonder who or what I have to thank.

The Queen of Cups

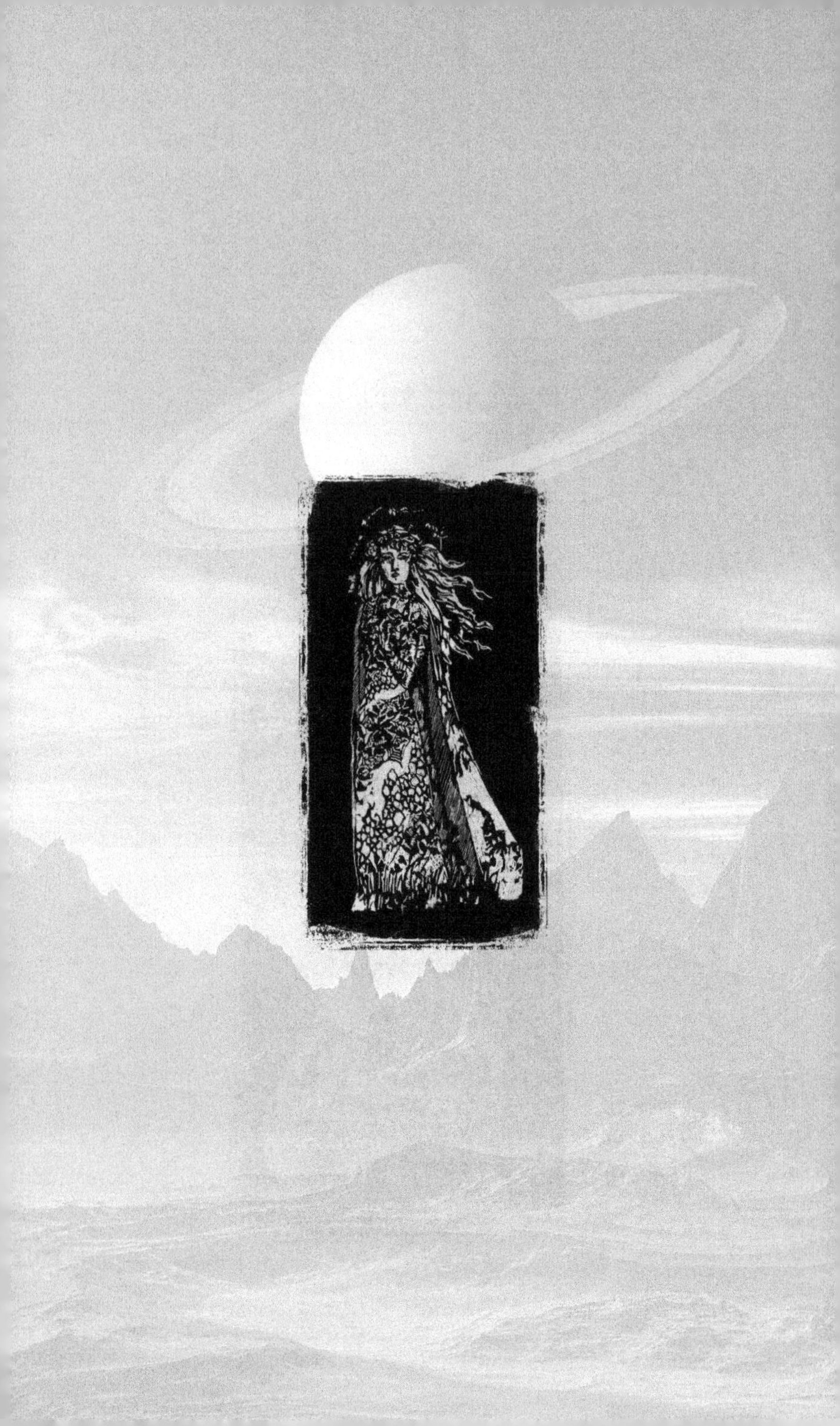

The Queen of Cups

By evening, the intense heat had become more tolerable. Dia wanted to move around, to walk, they'd had yet another day unable to move in the sweltering heat. He was used to heat too, back home in Nigeria, but Earth had just the one yellow sun. Lying down in the shuttle was marginally better than lying down in its shade outside as the heat shields prevented it from becoming an oven, but they couldn't waste fuel on air conditioning so had to keep the doors open. But at dusk there was a slight respite from the unrelenting suns which now looked like melting gold beyond the green horizon.

Dia looked north over the cliff to the grey stone plains beyond. The rock had been cut into and quarried on some massive scale. The right angles of the sliced plains was almost too much to take in. It was an impressive sight, even just in three-dee, he thought.

They'd dated the quarry to an age of around 20,000 years, at a guess as there was no organic matter around for carbon analysis and no rainfall to measure erosion. So the estimate was from atmospheric corrosion alone. They'd no idea who had quarried the rock or what they'd done with it. Yet. Their forthcoming trips up dee might show more.

Samita called his name from the shuttle, 'Dia? Supper.'

His compatriots had set up a table just outside the bay doors lit by the shuttle's light, although there were electric candles on the table. All the electric tools were powered by solar, charged up during the day. All except the air conditioning, annoyingly.

Samita had cooked a fine curry again. The four of them tucked in. There was Chen, he was the project leader, very considered, serious and very much the intellectual. Samita had the greatest scientific mind of them all. It was her research into dee levels that had made these dimensional surveys possible and it was an honour to actually have her with them instead of one of her apprentices. Klair was the technician, the engineer. She made things work. And then there was Dia, the artist. The one who had to make sense of all that was to come.

After supper Klair produced a pack of cards.

'Poker?' said Chen.

'No. Tarot,' said Klair. 'I'll do the Celtic cross. Who's up for a reading?'

'Do Dia,' suggested Samita. So Dia it was.

Klair shuffled the pack of well worn coloured picture cards, 'These were my grandfathers. You're allowed to touch the pack once, just for the final shuffle, then hand them back to me,' she said.

Chen took the cards and clumsily shuffled the deck briefly before handing them back. Klair took the top card and laid it face down horizontally on the table in front of her.

'That's the denominator,' she said, turning the card over, 'which will colour the reading. It's The Priestess which means a subtle connection with the collective unconscious, seclusion and self reliance.' She then laid out further cards, all face down in the shape of a circle with a cross through it. 'Each position on the cross has a meaning which each card will help us gain some insight. So let's begin.'

Klair turned over each card in a sequence, explaining each position and the meaning of the card in connection with it. Then there were three cards left.

'This represents your environment and unseen forces influencing the situation,' she turned over the card to reveal the Lovers. 'It indicates a connection on a higher level, mutual understanding and deep emotions. This penultimate card is your hopes and fears regarding the situation.' The card revealed was The Fool. 'These are all major archana, powerful forces which indicate change. I see in this spread a great change to do with you being found after not realising that you've been lost.'

The others had been watching intently. No-one had spoken since the reading had begun. They'd all been drawn in by Klair's performance. Sometimes they didn't need to talk anyway. The very nature of the project had made them all closer than anyone ever could be.

'The final card is the outcome of the situation. I believe it will show us what you will find, or rather what will find you.' She turned over the final card. It was The Queen of Cups.

'What does it mean?' Asked Dia, now impatient for a conclusion to the story.

'I didn't expect that. I'm not sure,' said Klair. 'It indicates, many things, an acutely sensitive woman, with powerful intuition, strength, integrity. It can mean love and a happy union. We have a predominance in the spread of the suit of Cups which is itself a strong feminine source.'

'Thanks Klair,' said Dia. 'Very interesting.'

'OK,' said Chen, his politeness holding back his inherent skepticism. 'So how is it supposed to work? Are you expecting us to believe there is some intelligence manipulating the choice of cards to communicate some sort of prophetic message?'

'I believe there is an intelligence at work,' said Klair. 'I think it's the subject's own.'

'You're saying I read into the meaning of the cards and what you've said, to make up something I wanted to hear?' said Dia.

'Partly,' continued Klair, 'but not necessarily what you wanted. It's more the case of your subconscious looking for relevant meaning in the apparent randomness of the cards.'

'So you don't believe in, I don't know, 'the supernatural'?' said Dia.

'You know as well as I do that there is only nature,' said Klair.

'And God,' added Samita. 'Let's get some sleep. We need to be up at dawn and get onto plus one before it gets too hot. Klair, help me prepare everything for the morning.'

The two of them got the equipment ready, the syringes, cortex caps and diagnostics. Dia and Chen cleared up the supper table.

At dawn, after a brief breakfast, they loaded up backpacks and began the short journey down the cliffs to the quarried plain. They unloaded their packs in the centre of the flat grey slate-like area, still some distance from the opposite stone cliff. Size and scale were deceptive. Klair assembled various block sections of electrical equipment into the diagnostic station. Samita got the three cortex caps ready. Three because she would not be participating in the survey. Someone had to remain in three-dee to monitor things. She reached into her pack to produce three hypodermic needles, loaded with a clear liquid. The other three took their stabilisation tablets and put their caps on.

Dia knew the preparation process was painless but he still felt a twinge of fear as to the unknown they were about to face. The injections were administered. They contained a mix of a number of psychoactive narcotics and stimulants. The rubber caps they wore on their heads were mounted with electrode stimulation probes. These were controlled by the diagnostic unit which sent various pulses to both activate and sedate various alternating parts of the cap wearer's cerebral cortex.

What would happen next would only ever work on less than one percent of the population. The perceptual filters that constrained, filtered and processed everyday sensory input would be scrambled. Only a further one percent of the one percent of people would then be able to make sense of the new reality that the subject would be faced with. Very few were able to re-order this multi-dimensional data using the hitherto unknown tenth sense.

It was the discovery of this 'tenth' sense that Samita was involved with. For centuries people had thought human senses were fixed at nine: vision (ophthalmoception), hearing (audioception), touch (tactioception), taste (gustaoception) and smell (olfacoception) are the most familiar. The inner ear that senses balance and acceleration including gravity is known as equilibrioception. Thermoception is the sense of temperature. Nociception is the sense of pain and finally Proprioception is the sense of our limbs in relation to each other.

The tenth sense, even after it was discovered, had been difficult to define. It was first described as the ability to be aware of dimensions. In normal life we take our three-dee world for granted and we don't realise that we are labelling it as three-dee. We know we can perceive and move in length, breadth and height. It was only when people entered the four and five-dee worlds that it was discovered that some humans were able to process and quantify the extra dimensions in just the same way someone with perfect pitch knows the difference between the notes E, F and G or that anyone with normal vision can tell the difference between yellow, red and blue, and would never get them confused.

Samita was controlling the diagnostic controller, sat on a portable chair. The others were just standing together. The caps were wireless so there was nothing restraining them.

As they stood there in silence, Dia thought about how strange it was to pass through the first two extra dimensions. Although they called them simply four and five, they'd acquired the names 'within' and 'without' due to the way the human mind processed them. Breadth was of course at right angles to length, turning a line into a closed shape by adding a dimension. Height was at right angles to both of those turning a closed shape, like a square, into a cube. 'Within' was at right angles to all three, creating a hypercube. If that was hard enough to explain, then 'without' at right angles to all of those four, was even harder to visualise, creating a megacube. Perceiving these dimensions was too difficult to describe and process by the human mind which is why they aimed to pass through them as quickly as possible, to minimise the disorientation they triggered. The goal was to run their dimensional survey within the sixth dimension, the first of the 'ultra' dimensions they imagined existed, although no-one had moved up to a seventh. But mathematically it had been proved that there were at least fourteen.

It had begun. They were entering the fourth dimension. Closing one's eyes was no use as equilibrioception gave the feeling of being upside down. Even though Dia knew his feet were on the ground, he could no longer tell which way was down, everywhere appeared to be up and down. In the fourth dimension, nothing was closed. You could see within everything. It was like suddenly being stood in a room in a house and then being given a plan of the house where you could now see inside each and every room from above at the same time as being inside one of the rooms. The reality of this was weirder. He could now see within everything and everyone. He looked over at Samita. She was no longer a closed unit. He could see her organs, her blood, her brain. It was the same for all of them. His friends looked like they had all been opened up on a dissecting table, and the organs revealed had been opened up, and the cells within had been opened up and the molecules that made the cells had been opened up to reveal atoms like discs of coloured cellophane. He could sense the electrons in the diagnostic machine, they felt like spinning rods, like single, very thin blade propellers. He could hear their spin which sounded like a short looped delicate melody.

They were moving up to the fifth dimension. Dia knew now to keep very still. His sense of proprioception had been absorbed into all things as they entered 'without'. There was no difference now between him and the others, between him and the rock. It was as if he and his colleagues, and the world had become spread out onto a continuous sheet of paper. He saw Samita's childhood home in India. He heard her grandmother speaking to her in Urdu. He knew it was different to English but he understood it. He felt the pain of Klair's parents divorce back in Ireland. It had been Christmas. There was snow. He'd never seen snow for himself but could feel its chill and its beauty through Klair's experiences. Chen had been an international traveller all his life. Although he came from China, grew up in Singapore and Malaysia, he'd studied at Yale and Oxford. Dia felt his restlessness. He felt a longing to stop moving. And yet Chen had chosen this life of space travel. Dia felt part of them all, and them part of him, their thoughts were his thoughts and theirs his. This is why he had been chosen for this mission. His skill as an artist would be shared with the others from this point. They would interpret the world as he would. Dia had become not just an artist, but the art himself.

Then they were through. They had arrived in the ultradimension, number six. Here, their brains were able to filter all their perceptions out once again and formulate a world view that was fairly stable and manageable. The sickness feeling had gone. He was aware of the others inside him and he in them but it was controllable just as you can choose to ignore someone who's talking to you even though you can never turn your hearing off.

The three of them looked around at the landscape. In ultra, they couldn't really communicate with Shamita. Effectively she resembled a chalk drawing on the ground. They spoke to each other in thoughts, not words. Although their perception had been normalised by their brains, Synesthesia remained. Colours made noises, so as they looked around, different tones filled their ears. Dia looked up at the sky. It was a pulsating mass of a two colour tonal pattern, like a pulsating optical illusion. The twin suns were still there, although they looked black against the bright sky, but to look at them directly was unbearable due to the impossibly loud noise coming from them.

But the most dramatic change was all around. They no longer stood in a featureless grey quarry but in a felled clearing in an enormous forest. The air was filled with tiny moths or hornets, whose silent buzzing was a kaleidoscope of changing colours. Sawdust and remains of purple tree trunks lay about. In the distance, near where the terraced rock cliffs had been, was now a thick cherry red forest of trees, their delicate song drifting across the barren dusty waste. There were a few ugly machines scattered about, abandoned. Chrome plated cutting machines that snarled and hissed in silence.

'It's wrong,' thought Dia. 'Something's is wrong here. This is wrong.' He started moving off in the direction of the forest.

'We mustn't move!' thought Chen. 'We must remain. It's dangerous to move.'

But Dia felt a cyan taste in his gut. It said 'come'. He began to move.

As far as Samita was concerned, nothing had happened at all. No-one had spoken and no-one had moved a muscle. The three of them had just stood there, looking out, with their caps on as the suns rose in the sky and the heat increased. Most of the time she'd been monitoring the controls on the diagnostic. She took a swig of water from a bottle. Then she saw Dia move off. He had begun walking slowing away towards the uncut cliff. The other two did not move. Shamita knew this was irregular. She returned to the controls to bring them back to three-dee. It would take some time so as to not cause sickness, or worse. But Dia had broken into a run. He was an athletic figure and a fast runner.

Klair and Chen saw him disappear into the forest just as they dropped down out of ultra into the fifth and then the fourth dimension. Then they were aware of Shamita, working frantically at the controls. They were back in three-dee.

'What's going on?' said Chen, removing his cap.

'I don't know. Why did he move?' said Shamita.

'We don't know. We couldn't hear him anymore. He seemed to float away,' said Klair.

'What's he doing over there?' said Chen. They could still see him in the distance. 'He must have dropped down to normal by now. The cap range isn't that big is it?'

'No, it's not. But look at this,' said Klair.

The diagnostic display showed no attachment subjects. No caps were registering.

'So he's back?' said Samita.

'Then what is he doing over there?' said Chen. 'We better get after him.'

Dia had entered the forest. There was a sound of turquoise all around the purple trees with their cherry red leaves. He could also hear the singing of the moth or hornet bee creatures. The wood became thicker and slightly darker or quieter. He moved slowly forwards until he came upon a clearing. In the centre was a tiny lake, or perhaps a wider part of a stream that flowed across his path.

Upon the other bank upon what looked like a golden throne sat a beautiful woman. In her hands she cradled a cup with handles shaped like angels. She wore a gold crown and silver robe. Her bare feet did not touch the water, they rested on colourful rocks washed up in front of her.

'You came,' said the woman.

'I had to,' said Dia.

'I know you Dia. Do you know who I am?' she said.

'No, I do not,' he said.

'I am Innana, Isis, Titania, Aroha. I am your queen,' she said.

'I do know you. I thought of you with the cards, you are the final card, the six of cups.'

'I am,' she said. 'I chose those cards for you. I chose your path for you. I chose your name for you. I've been following you, guiding you Dia, all your life. I've been in love with you Dia, since before you were born.'

'How can that be possible?' said Dia. 'Where are we, where is this place?'

'This is the forest of Eden, Aaru, Nariphon, the Cedar forest, Hercynia, Mag Mel, Avesta, the fields of Elysia,' said the woman. 'I called you here, across the skies. We are to make new life Dia. We are to have children. I've waited for so long for this moment Dia. My people are gone, betrayed. We will begin again.'

Dia's mind raced. But somehow it made sense. He got it. This trans-dimensional species reproduced in this way. He had become part of some pan-dimensional mating ritual. She was some kind of queen bee, some kind of creature that had hunted him, called him, created or caused him. But Dia did not feel used. There had been a terrible thing here. A genocide. The quarrying had killed her people. It was an honour to be chosen, to resolve this crisis, to continue a species. He only felt adoration and love for this woman.

'We shall be the seed! We shall be the New! Come my love!' said she.

Dia came.

They raced over to where Dia's body lay. He was alive, dehydrated and unconscious.

'Let's get him back to the shuttle,' said Chen.

They each took a limb and lifted him up.

It was nightfall. Back in the ship they had failed to revive him, but he was on a drip and looked stable. Chen was getting the shuttle ready for take-off. His main concern was not particularly Dia. Did they have enough data to have made the trip worthwhile? The company would need to know. First the shuttle would dock with the ship. Then the ship would translate back to Earth. Even hyperspatial travel would take them a few weeks to get back. Chen checked through Samita's logs and discussed the findings with Klair. Even with the incident with Dia it looked like they had more than enough to take back to Earth.

Etched onto the bark of the trees Dia saw shapes, regular shapes. He distantly recognised them as the schematics of the shuttle. There was also diagrams of the DNA of his compatriots from Earth, their faces and their systems. He stood hand in hand with the Queen. Both hands in both hands. She was inside him. He was her. Dia had had relationships before, he'd had intercourse before. But he'd never made love, not like this. He'd never become one. There was no Dia, there was no Queen. Now there was just We. There was just We and there was the Plan. They tried to stop us, but they had failed. We laughed. They came here with their machines to cut the forest and destroy us, contain us. Oh how We suffered, We nearly lost all but We had the Plan. They didn't know who We were. They didn't know the Plan!

Then, the forest was gone. We felt a tang of sadness as our home became a weaker gravitational field and all that was around was photons an the probability shells of a few electrons. Somehow We knew that the shuttle had taken off into the shine of space. We were on our way to Earth.

Now there was just the glorious Plan and it was well underway.

Magic Mirror

On the Shores of Lake Onyx and other weird tales

Magic Mirror

'Once upon a time there lived a wicked goblin who built a magic mirror. Anything that was beautiful or good was reflected in it as ugly and bad. The goblin wanted to fly with it up to heaven to show God and the angels, but the higher he flew the more slippery the glass became and it slipped from his hands and fell to the earth, and was broken into millions of pieces...'

Such is the introduction to Hans Christian Anderson's 1845 story of *The Snow Queen*. Magic mirrors in fairy stories seem commonplace. The evil queen consults one that talks back to her in the Brothers Grimm's story of *Snow White*. But aside from those and the entertaining distorted mirrors in fairgrounds, the looking glasses in real life tend to reflect exactly what is shown before them. Curious then that there are other stories, in different places and in different times, that I have have come across and drawn together, of mirrors with different, unnatural and distasteful properties. More than that I came to a conclusion that these scraps of tales may well refer to the same object, a very singular mirror which by all accounts sits at the centre of some queer occurrences. I will attempt to give a brief summary of these accounts before detailing my own research and the mistakes I made which led me to track down this mirror and foolishly bring it into my possession.

There are these few and very short apocryphal stories, more like hearsay that refer to a looking glass with remarkable features. The earliest account I came upon is a story set in the Court of Chetel, who was a Norse Lord during the rein of Edward the Confessor. It was said that Chetel would consult a looking glass to see which of his knights would not be returning from battle. His 11th century estate was demolished and rebuilt as Chatworth House by Bess of Hardwick in 1553.

Another story involves Henry VIII who is said to have gazed into a mirror to see images of his deceased wives. According to this story, each woman Henry had married appeared, stood behind him in the glass, except for Catherine of Aragon and Anne of Cleves. The story does not definitively say where the mirror hung although it may have been at the home of Sir John Burghersh, at his Manor of Ewelme in Oxfordshire where Henry would often visit. On Sir John's death in 1491, the house had passed to his younger daughter, Maud, who had married Thomas Chaucer, son of the poet Geoffrey Chaucer. Curiously, a mirror features in Chaucer's Canterbury Tales in the unfinished *The Squire's Tale* which tells of a strange knight who visits Genghis Khan with a variety of magical gifts including a mirror which can reveal the minds of the king's friends and enemies.

These snippets of stories, all referring to mirrors, stand alone and yet there appears to be a connection between them in that they all sit in and around large country estates with the Midlands. I took this as a clue to them perhaps referring to a single artefact, passing from one house to another.

Mirrors, magic or otherwise were never really to the forefront of my mind until I became aware of a particular object that might fit such a description by accident. A friend of mine's great aunt had died and there was a variety of obscure items put up for sale from her Derbyshire manor house. I had little interest at first, being more of a student of antiquities rather than antiques, but Johns had persuaded me to take a look at a singular painting he had pulled from the auction for himself. His great excitement about the picture was unusual enough to pique my curiosity and I travelled to Evesham in Worcestershire to take a look.

Johns lived in a modest farmhouse, probably late sixteenth century, low ceilings and with many, yet small fireplaces. With inset oak beams there was not the wall space to house the large frame that he unwrapped excitedly and placed on the dining table. The frame was dark wood, elaborate but ugly. The mount was mottled with age and exposure to damp. Johns fetched a cloth and some vinegar to wipe the grime from the glass and then held the picture up. It was portrait in orientation which wholly unsuited the subject matter of the actual image. The painting, in oils, showed an odd view of the corner of a room with the open oak door to the room in the corner on the left wall. To my eyes it was clearly the work of an amateur and at first I could not think why Johns had found such excitement in such a dull depiction. Mounted on the wall on the right was a mirror, probably around the same size as the picture itself, hung on its longest edge, which was around three feet across, from a high picture rail. The mirror's frame, like the coving and high ceiling above, was gilded quite elaborately. The room's walls were red. The floor was unusual, covered in large black and white chequered tiles. It was a strange perspective to chose to paint, with all the dramatic angles of the room pointing towards the empty centre of the painting, in which very little was to be seen. The interest lay in the mirror itself for reflected in it was some of the rest of the room; a small table with a vase, a column with a carved head and a cross hung on the wall which could be seen both on the wall and in the reflection in the mirror. But, also there in the reflection, and only in the reflection, was a hooded figure whose face could not be seen but from whose position it was obvious that the figure giving the reflection should have stood in the centre of the painting by the door, directly facing the viewer of the painting.

'What do you think?' Johns asked.

'It's quite grotesque, but clever. It took me a while to spot the figure at first,' I replied. 'What's its provenance?'

'It hung in one of Aunt's spare guest rooms. I don't think anyone ever went in there. I certainly didn't.'

'But what's it a picture of?' I said. 'Is it one of your aunt's rooms?'

'No,' said Johns, 'but I have a clue about the mirror. Someone at Aunt's house once told me a story about a mirror that revealed more than it should. I wondered if it could be the same. How do you feel about a visit to the Ashleian museum back in Oxford?'

Johns laid the picture down again. It was then that I noticed another detail in the reflected hooded figure. It appeared to be holding, in a gloved hand, a blade behind its back.

Although a fascinating treasure trove, which I knew very well, our visit to the Ashleian gave us only a further clue rather than the artefact itself. There had indeed been a mirror fitting our description gifted to the museum some while ago. There was a record of its arrival and a catalogue number. But when our curator went to retrieve it, he found only a note saying that it had been removed for cleaning and restoration by a certain Mr Forester in 1881. I made a joke about the efficiency of this man, taking twenty years to do what should have been a few days work. We did gain the address of this Forester gentleman and since it directed us the heart of the Cotswolds, to Stow-on-the-Wold, not far away, we set off that very day to hope beyond probability that the trail of the mirror would not go cold.

The weather however had turned cold and the first snows of the season arrived, causing it to be well into the evening when our trap arrived at the seventeenth century Unicorn Inn. We took the opportunity to discuss our mission with the proprietor. Forester, he revealed, had passed away nearly twenty years previously. His wife and son lived at the same address as in our information and were still in the same business of carpentry and the restoration of furniture.

There was hope.

The next day we set off on foot through the light snow that had fallen in the night. Forester's cottage and workshop was just on the edge of the town and easy to find. His son was out on business and Mrs Forester was initially pleased to accept us. When talk turned to the mirror, her tone changed. Yes, she had seen it.

'I curse the day that I set eyes on that evil abomination. Made by the devil himself that looking glass was,' she said.

'What became of it?' I asked.

'It was the day before Fredrick passed. It made me so disturbed I wrapped it up in a cloth and put it in the cellar. I daresay it's still down there but I wish it weren't,' she said.

We discussed a payment but she refused.

'I've not known what to do for the best with it,' she said. 'I don't want anymore bad luck from it and I don't want no money from it. No-one profits from... that.'

Johns left a pound note on her kitchen table anyway, 'Not for the mirror, for Christmas,' he said.

'I'll say just this,' said the woman, 'that you not unwrap it here. I do not wish to look upon that thing again.'

We agreed to this simple instruction and left. Outside Johns told me of a superstition to cover mirrors after a death so that the devil may not capture the soul of the deceased. Since my rooms in Magdalen were nearer than John's cottage, we returned there, eagerly awaiting the big reveal of the unwrapping.

Pausing to light a fire and our pipes, we finally attended to the object itself. Unwrapping the blanket that surrounded it was the job of a moment and the mirror was at last revealed. After the thrill of the hunt, our actual quarry was itself quite disappointing. Far from being a silvered mirror it was almost entirely matt, speckled and tarnished. It was very hard to make out anything in the reflection. You would not even recognise your own face in the distorted mottled surface. The cracked wooden frame was in places still partly coated in flaked gold leaf. The frame, although very old, was clearly not of the same antiquity as the glass itself.

'It's rather a let down,' I said.

'Oh I don't know,' said Johns. 'I can see it working a little like looking for patterns in tea leaves or sheep entrails. The mirror is so dishevelled and fogged I'd wager you could imagine seeing all sorts of images in it. Although I can't see how anyone could have taken this seriously as a portent,' he added. 'Either people were more gullible in the past or they were just having a bit of a wag.'

We had dinner in hall and I found Johns a room to stay over until the next day. Although I had almost considered the hunt over and the matter closed, he still wanted to pursue the origination of his great aunt's painting, which had started us off on the quest in the first place. So after breakfast he set off back to Derbyshire to attempt to follow the trail of the painting back before his aunt's ownership with the hope of tracing its origins and perhaps more about the story of the mirror itself.

It was almost a week later and I had returned to my normal business when I considered that I hadn't heard from Johns for a while. At that moment I caught sight of the mirror once again, leaning against the wall on top of the bureaux where I'd left it a few days earlier. It seemed to glisten. The more I looked, the more the blurred fog seemed to clear until I saw, reflected back in it perfectly, my own face and the room behind. I pondered this change for a moment, wondering if we had before just looked at the mirror with the wrong lighting, the wrong angle, or if our attempts to polish the glass had brought about some delayed effect. Then, some sudden noise caused me to look behind me over my shoulder. With no evidence of anything there I turned back to the mirror to see a second visage, a second figure, stepping out from behind me. There in the glass was my reflection as before but stood behind me, staring blankly into my eyes from the mirror was the face of my friend Frederick Johns. I whirled round, half expecting him to have crept up behind me, although I knew well that he must still be in Derbyshire. Behind me was no-one. I was alone in the house. Turning back to the mirror, Johns' face was no longer there. Neither was my own. The mirror had returned to its previous appearance of the whitish and brown stained metallic dull lustre.

The unexplainable episode clearly left me concerned for Johns. All I could do was send a telegram. A day later a letter came from him in the post, but it had been sent a few days before my telegram. An edited transcript of the relevant parts follows:

'My dear Robert. Although I have failed to find the actual room in the painting, I believe I perhaps have the answer to that which has eluded us thus far. My great aunt's picture did indeed once hang at Hardwick and there are servants here old enough to remember it. They also have a compelling back story for the mirror.

'In late 1095 a hooded figure, later revealed to be an agent of Emicho of Flonheim, entered a house in Mainz on the Rhine, a Roman fort city in the Holy Roman Empire, and brutally murdered a wealthy family including seven young children. The murder was designed to be blamed on the Jewish community, marking the beginning of the persecution of Jews, a factor in the run up to the first Crusade, linking the idea that both Jews and Mohammedans must be converted to Christianity or die. Interestingly enough, the family were German master craftsmen whose skill lay in the making and coating of blown lead glass with a tin-mercury amalgam to make the first ever high quality large flat mirrors. It is said that long after the Crusades had begun, a boy looked into a certain mirror from that house which depicted the scene of the massacre.'

I was interrupted from pondering this story by a knock at the door. It was the postboy. He handed me a telegram. It had a black border. He didn't wait for a reply. I opened and read the following message:

'Dear Robert thank you for your telegram (Stop) Henry passed away 15th December following a traffic accident (Stop) Funeral 22nd at St Mary's (Stop). Yours Cecilia Johns.'

I felt sick. Johns' death was the very day I had seen his face in the mirror. Just like in the stories I'd so far collected with glee, I realised that now I too had seen a vision in that accursed object of a man who was about to die. I couldn't bare to be in the same room as the diabolical object. I went to pack it up and remove it, but in my frustration, anger and fear, I'm afraid to say I reached instead for a heavy log from the fireplace and used it as a projectile, launching it at the cursed mirror with all my strength. The ancient glass, of course, splintered with a terrific crash. It had broken into seven pieces. I swore under my breath for doing such a destructive and irresponsible thing. I'm not a superstitious man, but the idea of the Roman myth of 'seven years bad luck' came into my mind. I resolved to completely destroy the mirror, thinking that might mitigate the possibility of misfortune. I flung the pieces into the fire, realising again too late that the fire was of course nowhere near the temperature to melt glass, but at least would strip the glass of its metallic coating, thus destroying its ability to be a mirror. The flames of the fire turned blue-white then bright red as they licked around the broken shards, burning up the tin and mercury. I picked up the tongs with the aim of removing the blackened pieces and burying them very deep in the ground as the superstition tells us is necessary to protect against the bad luck. But as I looked, each piece was not blackened but instead were shiny and clear. Each piece shone and glinted in the flames as perfect mirrors. I peered closer, looking directly at the largest piece which had landed side on, sitting upright in the blaze. The image in it was crystal clear. In it I saw my own face once again. Then, as before, I saw in the glass another figure step out of the shadows from behind me. I knew without looking around that there was no-one else in the room. The figure stepped to the side and moved forward so there was no disputing exactly who it was. I stared in horror at the two figures reflected back at me from the piece of glass in the flames. I stifled a scream. Next to the reflection of my own face, was another rendition of… myself.

The Moth

On the Shores of Lake Onyx and other weird tales

The Moth

I was disturbed from my book by a soft fluttering sound. The light from the reading lamp had attracted a small moth. Just one moth, but there could perhaps soon be others, so I closed the window. It was during the first heatwave of early July and the air was humid. The window really needed to be open. One moth. I could deal with one moth, if it would just stay still for a moment so I could catch it under a cup and release it outside, or even in the hall where I could not hear its flutterings. It did not stay still. It fluttered and repeatedly banged itself against the ceiling. I decided the leave it where it was and return to my book.

The story was based around a form of insomnia, an image that haunted a man and finally drove him mad. The moth continued to flutter with renewed vigour after a brief pause on top of the wardrobe. I found I was no longer able to concentrate and instead, frustrated, observed the moth as it settled just beyond my reach and crawled across the ceiling before resuming its random fluttering motion. Then, without warning, it flew directly at my face. I jumped back. Looking around, I saw the moth was now inside the conical shade of my reading lamp, its flutterings accompanied by the ping as its wings struck the metal shade. Dust motes floated down making the lamp's rays visible for a moment. I wondered how many moths end their days roasting in the heat of such lamps. Then the cruel thought came to me. I slowly lowered the lamp down onto the desk, plunging the room into darkness, only a glow from the ring of light, like an eclipse, where the lamp faced the surface of the desk. The moth was inside. The heat from the lamp burnt my hand. The fluttering stopped. I lifted the shade. There was the moth on the desk, still. Then, weirdly, I thought I saw two tiny objects scuttling away from it. They disappeared under some papers on my desk. Fleas? I lifted the papers. Then just for a moment I saw them. They looked like tiny, tiny men. Barely two millimetres tall. Then they were gone. I looked back to the moth. There was what looked like a tiny ladder descending from its abdomen. It dawned on me. This was no insect. I raced into the other room, to a drawer that I remembered putting a magnifying glass in. It was not there. I tried the kitchen drawer: nothing. The magnifying glass turned up in the bathroom cabinet. I returned to my study and the desk. There were my papers, the book, the lamp. But the 'moth' had gone.

Since that night I haven't been able to sleep. I know that they are on to me. They are watching me. They are watching all of us. I need you to believe me when I say that a large number of insect species are in fact vehicles piloted by the minute race known as the Salucidir.

I lie awake in the heat of the night. I lie there in the darkness, my lights are out. My windows are closed. In the heat and the dark, the silence is broken only by a tapping and a fluttering against the glass.

Secret of
the Circle

On the Shores of Lake Onyx and other weird tales

Secret of the Circle

'The signer hereby swears to the best of his knowledge and belief that no Jewish or coloured blood flows in either his or in his wife's veins, and that among their ancestors are no members of the coloured races.'

Such was the declaration to join the esteemed Thule-Gesellschaft society, founded in 1918 with the intention of researching the origins and historical supremacy of the Aryan race. On this particular document was the name 'Wolfram Sievers, 1928', signed in blood.

'Presumably it was his own blood?' I said as I handed the brown parchment back to Doctor Markus Reinhardt.

'No doubt,' replied the Doctor, 'But I believe the skin the parchment was made from was unlikely to be his. Probably Slavic. Sievers was hung in 1948. A Tibetan chant was performed upon his corpse.'

I'd got used to these ghoulish reveals from Reinhardt. Back in Munich I always thought he used them as techniques to filter out the squeamish or those with only a casual interest in Nazi history. He always talked of his predilection for 'purity', as if it was some kind of joke. But he was still employing his provocative methods here in

Oxford with me as the only research assistant left standing.

His unconventional approach to research had caused him to annoy almost anyone he'd come into contact with. There had been times when I worried my own Phd would collapse around me. But that was no longer a primary concern. Reinhardt's new discoveries and the connections I'd made myself pointed to the first tangible evidence of the mythical land of Hyperborea. It was Himmler's plan to preserve there either Nazi secrets, or more likely a division of crack troops, a leadership cell, or something.

Our theory was that whatever the secret of Hyperborea, it was to be activated in the event of Axis defeat in the war. Since that defeat had happened, over ten years ago now, something must have gone wrong. Or Hyperborea didn't exist. But our evidence was now so great that we were eager to begin the exploration. We knew something was waiting to be found.

Reinhardt had been to Iceland a few times before, following the war, studying ancient farming practices and architecture and to record local folksongs and dances. He had also collected soil samples for pollen analysis. Surprisingly well connected, he had managed to meet with Dr. Bruno Kress who wrote *Grammar of Icelandic* published earlier this year (before he began working for the Stasi in East Germany.) Reinhardt had all these quite useful, if not shady characters, at the end of a phone call or telegram.

Our expedition of course was quite expensive. I didn't ask where the money had come from. I knew it was not from the university, officially the trip didn't exist. Reinhardt did have dealings in Switzerland and had once joked about the irony of Nazi gold being used to uncover the Nazi's last great secret.

Heinrich Himmler's work with his exploration group, the Ahnenerbe, had postulated that it was the pure-blooded Aryan people of Hyperborea, part of an archipelagos of islands known as Atlantis, who had migrated to Germany. It was these Germanic people who had brought culture to the world, while a different evolutionary path had led to the sub-human race of Semites, or Jews, who brought only evil.

We were in the final stages of our research. The documents we had, which included Himmler's own version of Gerard Mercator's 1595 *Septentrionalium Terrarum North Arctic Projection* as well as coordinates from the Ahnenerbe of what purported to be the city of Ultima Thule, the capital of ancient Hyperborea. We had enough to begin.

The trip from England to Reykjavik was uneventful but tiring. After a difficult time converting enough Króna to charter our small plane, we were finally en route. Our destination was around 402 kilometres north-east of Iceland, one hundred and ninety-three kilometres north-east of the small Danish island of Jan Mayen just within the arctic circle.

It was April, so the temperature at ground level was likely to be just above freezing. The featureless dark sea occasionally teased us with icebergs, but eventually the tiny grey island we'd been looking for came into view. It was perhaps only thirty-two kilometres across, triangular in shape. We were heading for the low ground at the southernly apex. We landed the plane easily on rough flat land right on the rocky coast. There were six of us in the party. There was our hired pilot and his co-pilot, Hans (another German) and Peter Dickinson, a biologist that Reinhardt had enticed to come along.

It was cold, and the wind-chill made it feel even colder as we emerged from the plane. Some powdery snow clung to areas of the ground where the wind hadn't managed to blow it away. We stretched our arms and legs and walked down to the coast first. This was the place all right. I could feel it. Reinhardt knew it too. The otherwise craggy coastline had been augmented with a large concrete jetty that stretched out into the sea for fifteen metres or so. It could have served as a small harbour for quite large boats. Further east the sea lapped up against the gravelly shore which was strewn with large chunks of what appeared to be charred wood. From my distance it appeared to be from the wreck of a boat. The north eastern sky was dark, foreboding clouds advanced upon us.

Leaving the two pilots to secure and check over the plane, we walked along what seemed an obvious path, through a natural gap in the hedges and hillside. There, in the middle of a large flat gravely area were two hangers, the typical quick to erect air force design with the slopped corrugated iron roof. There was a large one and beyond that a smaller one. The large rusty steel bay doors at one end of the first one proved too difficult to open. Round to the side was a generator and tanks of diesel. Hans found another door along the side which was easily opened.

I don't know quite what I expected. Perhaps a barracks or typical military outpost facility. But what we found turned out to be quite different. The building was divided into rooms. The first was an office, but it was too dark to see more. Hans and Dickinson went back outside and managed to get the generator working quite easily. We then switched on the lighting and explored further.

There were sleeping and eating quarters with a kitchen and an office. The kitchen area had every cupboard door open or smashed. There was no sign of any food supplies. We continued into what appeared to be laboratories and medical bays. These rooms were a mess. There was broken furniture, instruments, glass and other equipment strewn everywhere. Hans joked it was like a barroom brawl. Then he stopped and called us over. Here was the first horror. Behind a bench, crumpled on the floor was an emaciated skeleton, partially clothed in just his underwear. There was no head or left arm. Dickinson picked up a broken chair leg and slowly turned the carcass remains over. From the front it looked like the body had been ravaged by an animal. On the floor were military dog tags giving his name as Commandant Rudolph Fendleman. We had just come come to terms with this grisly discovery when Reinhardt called us over to another corner of the room and another corpse. Again, the emaciated remains had no outer garments and no head. Dickinson examined the dead man's arm closely.

'Teeth marks, look,' he said.

'What attacked them? Wolves?' I asked. No-one knew.

Reinhardt showed no further interest in the bodies or even in discussing them. He seemed more restless than ever and began searching the benches and what drawers there were in the room.

'Let's try the other building,' Reinhardt said, as if we knew what he was looking for.

Again, the side door was open. The lights worked and we went in.

I had never been to Birkenau, but had seen enough pictures to suspect: an airtight room, observation slits, a central hole in the roof.

'A gas chamber?' said Reinhardt. From his tone I took it to mean this was not what he'd expected. 'But there's no processing station, no barracks, no crematorium?' he said.

'Burials?' I suggested.

'In this rocky ground?' Reinhardt said. 'And anyway, why bring prisoners here? Why bring anyone or anything here at all?'

The room had a distinctive slatted wall. I touched it's cold surface. It was entirely covered in strips of lead.

We returned to the other building. Dickinson and Hans examined the laboratories while Reinhardt and I examined the office. This room was not wrecked as the others had been. There were files and a few books on a shelf, a desk and three chairs. We looked through the drawers and at the files. Dickinson and Hans entered.

'Any clues?' I asked.

'We think so,' said Dickinson, 'There's been some vivisection here, certainly.'

'On people?' I asked hesitantly.

'No,' continued Dickinson, 'most likely on pigs. Ordinary farm swine. As well as some quite complex pharmacological work. Some serious chemistry went on in there.'

'What have you there?' Hans asked me.

'It looks like the camp records,' I replied, flicking through it. I read sections of it out. It appeared that the scientific base was set up during the summer of 1938 by the Ahnenerbe under Himmler's authority, although Himmler himself never visited. His own trip was cancelled due to the Battle of Britain in 1940. The mission it seemed was to purify the Aryan race through some programme of genetic experiments. 'But DNA wasn't discovered until 1952?' I said.

'No, that was the discovery of its structure, it was identified in 1944. Let me see,' said Dickinson.

I handed him the book and some other files.

'Yes, they were into genetics. Chromosomes had been identified as carrying genetic information since 1913,' he flicked through the many papers, 'They were interested in what made Jews different from Germanics. They thought there was a genetic difference and that the Germanic people had been corrupted by these Jewish genes... yes, here it says the idea was to purify contaminated Aryans and 'cure' Jews of their Jewishness by altering their genetic structure, or some such nonsense like that. They extracted the cell nuclei of pigs...'

'Why pigs?' I asked.

'There's a very high degree of similarity between the human and pig protein coding sequence' said Dickinson, 'they must have known that. Or perhaps they had some weird idea about injecting pig genes into Jewish people.'

'Look at this,' said Hans, 'Prisoner details. There were twenty prisoners brought here. Ten were Jews and ten a variety of others.'

'They were doing some sort of chromosome transplants,' continued Dickinson, 'But if pig tissue is transplanted into humans our immune system will mount a drastic rejection response as the human body will detect the antigen and attack it... No wait,' he carried on reading, 'they knew that and came up with a solution to stop tissue rejection by eliminating the gal-transferase gene. But how? What's this Reinhardt, I can't translate it, it says 'Vril'?'

'Where does it say that?' snapped Reinhardt, grabbing the files from Dickinson. He flicked through the pages.

'Vril' muttered Reinhardt, 'It all makes sense. The gas chamber. They weren't using it to kill, but to infuse. They put the prisoners in there and filled the chamber with a Vril in aqueous, gaseous form, like steam in a sauna, after doing the chromosome injections as Dickinson has said. Of course! That's how they did it! We need to search the labs again.'

It wasn't making much sense. But we searched through the laboratory and the medical bay once again. This time looking for any kind of chemical container that might contain something that could be this elixir. Most of the phials were broken. There was some acid and other obvious solutions left intact. I found a number of Geiger–Müller tubes. All but one were broken.

'Let me see,' said Dickinson. He found an electric socket and plugged the device in. A steady crackle of clicks came from the speaker. The lead on the tube was long enough to point around the room. The clicks grew more intense at one end of a bench. Dickinson opened a wooden box. Inside was a collection of rocks with embedded translucent pinkish crystals. The Geiger-Muller tube gave the most concentrated barrage of clicks when pointed at them.

'Pollucite, I think,' said Dickinson. 'A rare form of caesium ore, found only in certain parts of the Arctic rock. Dissolve this in hydrochloric acid and you'll get a caesium chlorate you can then reduce to get the metal.' Dickinson closed the box.

We'd searched everywhere. Then I noticed a metal canister on the floor with a screw top lid. I opened it. Inside were small crystals like copper sulphate but a darker blue. I sniffed. They smelt sweet. I showed my find to Reinhardt. He couldn't contain his excitement.

'This is it! This is what I've been looking for all these years!'

He put the canister in his backpack and we all returned to the office to discuss our next move.

Something caught Reinhardt's eye on the wall. 'Look,' he said, 'Here.'

'What?' I replied. We went over to see what he was pointing at. It was a chart on the wall, presumably a map of the island.

'This is where we are,' he said, pointing to the lower part of the triangular island shape, and this,' his finger slid to the centre of the island, 'is Ultima Thule!'

'What are you talking about?' I said

'That's where we'll find the answers!' he replied.

I'd never seen him so excited. We returned briefly to the plane to brief the pilots and pick up supplies. The pilots decided to wait in the office in the hanger, even after we told them of the bodies in the adjacent room. I didn't blame them. It was getting colder.

'So what happened to everyone who was here? Where are the scientists and where are the prisoners?' I asked Reinhardt.

'I believe we will find the answers at Ultima Thule,' he said.

So we marched north over rocks. The centre of the island would only be thirteen or so kilometres and the flasks of hot coffee and brandy kept us warm. Some snow flakes blew around in the wind. I don't know if even Reinhardt knew what to expect.

What we found wasn't clear at first. The moor-like terrain was strewn with rocks, large and small. In some areas we walked over just rocks for some time. Then, as we drew closer to the centre of the island, we came upon a slight raised hill, and circling it on top was a large megalithic stone circle. As we got even closer the sheer size of the stones became apparent. They were rough hewn and heavily eroded, one and a half to two metres wide and three to four metres tall. I counted twenty in all. To me it was an uglier site than even the dead men we found earlier. This felt like an evil place. The others had walked to the centre and stood upon a large flat stone that emerged only a few centimetres above the ground, roughly circular in shape with a diameter of three metres. We were all looking at what was carved in it. The shape was heavily eroded and very ancient. But it was unmistakably the sign of the Schwarze Sonne, the Sonnenrad; the Black Sun or Sun Wheel, the twelve spoked swastika. I'd seen pictures of it before in the Obergruppenführer Hall, the SS Generals' Hall in the castle of Wewelsburg.

The others were looking at scattered, rusty equipment. It looked like the remans of drilling machinery.

'Was this a mining operation?' I asked, 'What's the significance of it?'

'You know what Vril is?' Reinhardt asked.

'Of course,' I replied, 'a mythical life-giving elixir.'

'Not mythical,' said Reinhardt, still looking around at the ugly stones, and the broken bits of drilling and construction gear.

'What was that?' said Hans, startled.

'What was what?' I asked, looking around.

'A noise,' said Hans.

'Where's Dickinson?' said Reinhardt slowly.

We all looked about. He'd definitely stood in the circle with us. We looked around and called his name. Then came a scream which echoed through the circle. We rushed over to Hans. He couldn't speak and just pointed. There at the base of one of the stones was Dickinson. He'd had a massive blow to the head, his neck clearly broken, hung unnaturally. He was clearly dead, but sat up with his back to the megalith. He'd been put there...

We weren't alone. We slowly backed into the centre of the circle. Reinhardt and Hans both pulled guns from somewhere.
The snow was falling solidly now. It was hard to see much beyond the great grey stones.

Then we saw it. A uniformed figure lurched out of the white into our vision between the stones. It wore the jacket, cap and boots of a Nazi officer, but the rest of its garments were rags. As it lurched forwards we saw its face, a blank, staring, weatherbeaten pale white face. Parts of the cheeks were black from frostbite and it had no nose, or fingers. Hans and Reinhardt trained their guns on the advancing figure.

'What IS it?' I yelled.

'One of the prisoners no doubt,' said Reinhardt. We started to back away from the ghoul.

'But how can he be alive?' I said, 'Here all these years?'

The figure was slow, but still moving towards us.

'Because it's not alive!' said Reinhardt, 'It's untoten. Whatever their experiments were, they killed this man, but the Vril kept him from dying!'

Two shots rang out. Reinhardt had fired at the thing. It recoiled from the shots, paused, then continued its march. Hans fired too. The spectre stumbled and fell.

'Let's get out of here! Raus!' shouted Reinhardt.

But something else worried me. Did that monster kill Dickinson? If so, with what, and how did such a slow moving zombie get from Dickinson who was behind us, to be six metres in front of us?

My thinking process was too slow. A second fiend had grabbed Hans' neck from behind. Even without fingers it was able to throttle and scratch him. We tried to pull it off. I managed to get one arm off him, the creatures arm actually broke away and I fell back to the ground still holding it. Reinhardt emptied his gun into the beast. Both it and Hans fell to the floor. Hans was dead. We turned and fled the circle, clambering over the rough ground. At least we'd have speed on our side. But running over the rocks as the snow fell wasn't easy. Reinhardt slipped and sprained his ankle. He leant on me as we lumbered back as fast as we could, pausing only for a quick swig of brandy to keep us going.

Two hours it took us. Cold, tired and scared, we reached the clear area with the buildings at last and without further incident. But something else was wrong. It was too quiet. The generator must have stopped. I told Reinhardt to continue on to the plane while I fetched the pilots. It had stopped snowing, the fresh snow crunched underfoot as I approached the door to the building. The door was open. With no generator, the building would be in darkness...

I approached cautiously, cursing the snow for giving away my approach to anyone who might be listening. But there was another noise. A grunting, gurgling and gnashing noise coming from inside. It sounded like a large group of animals eating.

I panicked. I did not want to look inside that door. Instead I ran back to the shore and the plane. Reinhardt was waiting. He'd opened the canopy of the nearest plane. I didn't need to tell him why I had come alone. He looked tired, sleepy almost. I saw a gash on his face. It wasn't from when he fell. The creature must have scratched him.

'I'll be fine, let's get going,' he said.

Three of the bedraggled creatures appeared at the edge of the entrance to the hanger area. Their distorted faces were covered in blood.

'I hope to Gott in Himmel I can get this started, get in!'

But I couldn't get Reinhardt in the plane. He had collapsed. The ghouls were getting closer and closer. I tried to get Reinhardt onto my shoulders. His eyes opened briefly. They were glazed over. I could see the wound on his face was putrid. The lumbering creatures were almost upon us.

'The Vril...' he muttered.

I lowered him to the ground and fumbled in his backpack for the canister. But what to do with the crystals? Maybe they were soluble? Maybe he should swallow them whole? I got out what remained of the brandy and dropped a handful of crystals into the flask. It fizzed and frothed. I shoved the flask into Reinhardt's mouth. It seemed to give him strength. But the creatures were on top of us, one of them and knocked me to the ground. I saw at least a dozen more hobbling towards us, some wearing remnants of Nazi uniforms, a couple in orange boiler suits and the rest, the most disheveled ones, in just rags. One had grabbed Reinhardt and was dragging him off. Another picked up the hip flask and drank the contents, although holes in its chin meant most of the brandy dripped through to he ground.

There was nothing else I could do. The decision will haunt me for ever. Three of the zombies were crouched over Reinhardt, the others heading for me. Grabbing the Vril canister I climbed up to the cockpit. With a roar, the engine started first time and I quickly taxied around the area to attempt a big enough run for take off. I tried not to look back. I think I saw the group of creatures gathered round Reinhardt's body.

I'd trained as a pilot in the war and was able to get the plane to Keflavik military base in Iceland without too much trouble.

You know the rest. That is my complete statement.

The inspector looked up at Klaus and leaning back in his chair breathed a sigh.

'There's nothing in your story that convinces me that you didn't murder Reinhardt and the others. It was you who created this fabrication of a mythical island to gain access to Reinhardt's information on the Nazi bank accounts in Switzerland. You realise we will find the truth.'

'No!' shouted Klaus, jumping to his feet. Two officers

restrained him.

'What's more,' said the inspector, 'I think you must be sick, to make up such puerile junk as this. Walking, rotting dead men, injected with pig genes?'

'What about the Vril? You have the canister,' said Klaus.

'Sit down,' said the inspector.

Klaus sat down.

'Oh, we examined that canister of yours. The blue crystals? It's called Berlin Blue, or more correctly, ferric ferrocyanide. A common enough compound, used as an antidote for certain kinds of heavy metal poisoning, in particular caesium and thallium. You could have easily picked this up from any chemistry department at a university working with radioactive compounds.

'There's no such thing as Vril, except in the demented minds of Nazi occultists. Do you think we're stupid? It's a fabrication from a 1871 novel called *The Coming Race* by Edward Bulwer-Lytton. There is no such thing as Vril.'

Klaus said nothing.

'And as for your insinuations that Dr Markus Reinhardt was in some way complicit with the insanity of Himmler and antisemitism, you fail to have realised that Dr Reinhardt was an Austrian Jew. He fled Austria in 1936 and spent the war in Oxford before briefly returning to Munich where he was unfortunate to bump into you.'

'It's not true!' protested Klaus.

'We think you killed the men and dumped their bodies

somewhere to the north of Iceland. We'll get to the bottom of this. There is an expedition on its way to locate this magical island of yours as we speak, although the authorities in Iceland think, like me, that it's a total fiction.'

'No!' shouted Klaus, 'You mustn't! Don't you see? They must have burned their own boats when they'd realised what they'd done. They'd created a batch of mindless creatures that could not be killed, and whose contact caused a deadly infection. That's why the project was closed down. Even the Nazi's weren't stupid enough to let that happen. That's why they were abandoned and left to rot!'

'We'll get to the bottom of this. And you'll hang for the murders,' said the inspector. 'Take him back to the cells.'

The Fly

On the Shores of Lake Onyx and other weird tales

The Fly

Dust motes floated in a beam of sunlight. Beyond were a few figures, sat on a sofa and chairs.

'What was this place like?' asked Jim, holding a notebook and pen and not looking very comfortable on the sofa. Next to him sat his fellow student journalist, Bill.

'Just a house. An old house,' said Jack, an unsmiling man in his thirties. He was sat on an upright chair opposite them. He had a weary look, as though he hadn't slept for a long time. The room had a modern feel but was dark. On the mantelpiece were a number of incongruous objects including something carved from black wood and an animal skull. The room displayed a moderate wealth. It looked as though it had recently been re-decorated. The television and hi-fi were new and the latest technology, a bit too fancy for the rest of the house's standards, probably Bang and Olufsen. A clock ticked. There was the sound of a fly in the room.

Jack's wife Wendy placed three cups of tea on a small table unceremoniously. She glanced over to Jack and without smiling, left. Bill reached for a cup of tea, took a sip, found it too strong and held it awkwardly, waiting for the appropriate amount of time before he could put it back. The fly hovered over the cup, he swiped it away.

'It was dark, musty, old looking. There was an open fire. Bookshelves with leather bound books. All the furniture was old. The chairs were leather,' said Jack.

'What about the man. What was he like?' asked Jim.

'I don't know how old he was. He was old, but. I don't know. He wore a dark suit. I think he had a beard,' replied Jack.

Wendy hovered around in the doorway.

'What did he say?' asked Bill.

Jim looked over Jack's shoulder. There was a spider crawling across the wall.

'The man said he could help me,' Jack continued. 'Help me solve my problems. We talked. We talked for a long time.' Jack's sentences seemed to run out of steam, needing a constant prodding from the other two to get him to continue.

'What did you talk about?' asked Jim.

'Loads of things. Life. Luck. We discussed luck. You know, about winning and losing, in life. The man said his Master had the means to help me, financially. Make me lucky,' said Jack.

'His master? Who was he?' asked Bill.

Jim took a sip of tea and had trouble swallowing it. He looked around the room for the fly. The spider looked around the room for the fly.

'I don't know,' said Jack after an eternity.

'You didn't ask?' said Bill.

'At the time I didn't feel I needed to. It didn't seem important,' replied Jack.

The fly looked down on them all from above the window.

'Did you meet this man, the Master?' asked Jim.

'No. No I never met him,' said Jack. 'I didn't need to meet him. He said I'd meet him later, after.'

Jim looked at the animal skull on the mantelpiece. Was it a dog, a goat? There were too few teeth to tell. For a moment he thought the clock had stopped ticking. But no, it was ticking. The fly buzzed around somewhere above.

'So what exactly happened?' asked Jim.

'We agreed. Then I left,' said Jack flatly.

'And that's it?' said Bill.

The buzz of the fly became suddenly more intense. It was caught in a web.

'What did you agree? Did you, sign anything…' said Jim. The fly continued to struggle. '…in blood or anything?'

Bill gave Jim a funny look as if he'd overstepped the mark, said something that should have been left unsaid. The sound of the fly struggling stopped as the spider arrived at the web.

Jim looked at a knife on the mantelpiece. It was old and rusty with a carved bone handle.

'Well yes,' said Jack, 'There was the contract. It seemed fairly straightforward. I can't remember all of it. Not now. Then I left.'

'And now everything's fine?' asked Jim.

'Apart from…' came Wendy's voice from the doorway. A glance from Jack stopped her from finishing. She came further into the room, but stayed close to the doorway.

'We had problems. You know, serious problems,' she said.

'You owed people money?' asked Bill.

A car drove past the window. The clock ticked. Jack looked down.

'Yeah, that was it,' said Wendy at last, looking at Jack, never at Bill and Jim. 'We owed a lot of money. A lot of people a lot of money.'

'Yeah. That was it,' said Jim. 'But now everything's ok.'

'What, just like that?' asked Jim.

Wendy was clearly getting impatient, 'Just like that,' she said almost sarcastically. Bill and Jim felt that it was time for them to leave.

A few minutes later, nothing else of import had been said. Jim and Bill were outside the house and stood on a normal suburban street. Wendy watched them from an upstairs window, having pulled back the net curtain a little. The lounge window downstairs where they had just been appeared black.

'Sorry, I just couldn't wait to get out of there,' said Bill. 'You could cut the atmosphere with a knife.'

'It was making me feel giddy. Weird. Lets get away from here,' said Jim.

'The story?' said Bill.

Jim tore two pages from his notebook, 'There's no story here. No story anyone should want to hear. No story I want to tell.' He crumpled up the pages as they began to walk. After a few paces he dropped the paper into a bin.

The Glasshouse

On the Shores of Lake Onyx and other weird tales

The Glasshouse

Penelope Wilkins had been at the cottage two days before her duties at the main school house allowed her to explore the grounds. Most of the school masters lodged in the buildings within the old school but perhaps because she was a woman, she had been given a cottage, a little smaller than the others, set apart and slightly down a hill, within considerable land. It may have been the home of the groundsman in years gone by, Wilkins surmised. It was early January and the gardens were colourless and barren, and not just due to winter, it must have been many seasons before any care and attention had been given to the lawns, walled flowerbeds and the field beyond.

She was the first female teacher at this particular English boarding school, a small remote school on the coast. As a new mistress, Wilkins had been rather busy with a lot to learn and settle in. Like most schools, she had been given the bare minimum of information to get started and then had been left to 'get on with it'. So with a gap in her duties on her first weekend, Wilkins had a brief respite which allowed her to do a little exploring.

The cottage itself was cosy but unremarkable, so Wilkins aimed to walk through the gardens and see if a good route to the coast could be found. When the Hall had become a school, some time towards the end of the century, Victorian buildings had sprung up around it to accommodate the needs of a modern boys' boarding school. These had eaten up the grounds in unpredictable ways so that the cottage seemed to sit towards the edge of what must have been a larger ornamental garden, now mostly divided up and built on. But there remained a water feature, what may have been a rose arch and fruit tree avenues, all decrepit and overgrown now. Further on by the edge to the right was a low dry stone wall with a field beyond, used now as a paddock. It was a small matter to climb over this wall and stride through the field towards a striking and unusual looking feature not far away. It looked like a small, but perfectly formed hill, with some sort of structure on its flat top. Perhaps some sort of summerhouse or folly, thought Wilkins as she approached. It was round and about eight foot or so in diameter with a domed roof tapering up to a point in the centre. She thought it was painted a blue turquoise at first but on getting closer she was surprised to realise it was made entirely of glass. Climbing the small hill was no matter and in a moment Wilkins had reached the glasshouse and, walking around it, soon found the door to get in. The structure was metal framed with no pane of glass bigger than eight inches square in size. Many of the lead lined windows were much smaller. The floor was paved with smooth grey York stone. There was some sort of two foot diameter circular grate in the centre and various dusty and cracked plant pots scattered around with dried up contents including some long-dead plants.

Wilkins looked through the glass panes expecting to easily see the sea from this vantage point. It was difficult to make out much with any clarity. The glass seemed to be made of the most terrible quality.

It was uneven and distorting as well as giving the view a turquoise hue. Disappointingly, she saw some sort of building in the near distance obscuring the view. Various figures seemed to be moving about too. Farm hands perhaps? Although they looked a little odd, dressed in what appeared, through the distorting glass, to be in black hooded cloaks.

It was as she stepped out of the structure that she noticed the change in temperature first. It was unusually warmer outside the structure than it had been in it. Not a normal feature of a building made entirely from glass, even in the depths of winter. Once down from the small hill, Wilkins couldn't see the buildings or the people she'd seen in the distance. A glance at her watch told her she'd better return for lunch, which she did.

Wilkins attempted to get some details about the strange glasshouse from Adams, the headmaster. He didn't seem to have much to say or really be that interested, admitting he'd seen it but had never ventured up to it. A visit to the school library had furnished Wilkins with a map of the estate, as it was, which predated the construction of the school and the glasshouse by some years. Where it stood was the hill marked on the map as 'tumulus'.

'Found something interesting dear?' came a voice. It was Matron, a middle aged woman. 'You're interested in the history of this place, I see.'

'Well, yes,' said Wilkins.

'It's nice to have another woman around the place,' said Matron. 'Aside from me, there hasn't been a lady here since Lady Grimwade herself.'

'Lady Grimwade?' said Wilkins.

'She owned the school,' continued Matron. 'The Grimwades spent most of their final years travelling. They had no children. After her husband's death, Lady Grimwade became quite an eccentric recluse by all accounts.'

Being new, and being a woman, Wilkins felt cut off from the rest of the staff. There was one teacher, a maths master called Brownson, who was open enough to approach about the structure.

'A tumulus is, of course, a sort of barrow. They date from the late Neolithic, around three or four thousand years ago up through the Bronze Age.' he told her.

'What were they for?' asked Wilkins.

'To cover burials. Mainly for the rich and famous. Often a sort of man-made cave, covered over with soil and grass. I've seen the darn thing, but never bothered to go and have a look. Must pop down there sometime.'

It was a week later when Wilkins again had time for another explore of the glasshouse. The weather was much the same, clear skies and cold. Once inside the structure it was even colder. She pottered around inside, tapping a few of the cracked dried out plant pots with her boots. Then the centre grate caught her attention. It was about two feet wide, a circular disc formed from two hinged semi-circles. They were iron, and heavy to lift, but it was possible and Wilkins opened them both and they clanged down heavy on either side onto the stone flags. She peered into the dark hole and saw protrusions sticking out, like rungs of a ladder, leading down.

It was the work of ten minutes to go back to the cottage and return with a torch. Willings shone it down the hole. There appeared to be a solid floor some eight or nine feet down. She decided it was worth a look and the sides of the tunnel leading down looked solid enough to guarantee her return. Wilkins precariously began to lower herself down the hole.

She awoke with a freezing cold feeling on her left cheek. She was lying on the floor of the glasshouse. Lifting her head, confused, she looked through the bottom pane of glass of the structure. Through its blue, blurry translucency she caught sight of a figure, dressed in a black robe. Hooded. Carrying something long and pointed. Wilkins scraped herself up to her feet. Looking through the glass at head height she saw no figures. Dazed and bewildered she turned to look back at the centre of the structure. There was the grate, open as before and its dark hole. She patted her pockets. The torch was missing. What had happened? She opened the glasshouse door and peered out. There was no-one around. She returned to the hole once again. Had she imagined it? Remembering she had a box of matches, she lit one and peered down the hole. It was as it had been before. Convinced she must have somehow imagined her previous attempt and slipped before even attempting a decent, she lowered herself down the hole.

She awoke with cramp in her left leg. Once again she was lying on the cold floor and in the same place. Jumping up to her feet to relieve the pain she was shocked to not only be convinced that she had attempted to enter the hole just moments before but noticing to her horror that it was now totally dark. She was still in the glasshouse. Looking out through the glass it was night time. Outside she could see figures in the middle distance, near the structure that she'd noticed before, obscuring the sea, walking in a line with lit flickering lanterns. It was hard to resolve detail through the imperfections of the glass. No, not lanterns, fire torches. She raced to the door and stepped out. Standing on the grass on top of the mound she could see no figures. No lights. It was too dark to see anything at all in that direction. Behind her, beyond the field and wall were the lights of the school buildings. She nipped back inside the structure once more to look through the glass. This time she saw nothing through there either. She left the glasshouse and returned back to the cottage, confused and a little afraid.

Brownson accompanied her on her next visit to the glasshouse. Wilkins had explained some of her adventure, but not the mysterious inability to venture down the hole for fear of appearing deluded or weak.

'Very interesting indeed,' said Brownson, looking into the structure from the outside. 'What's it made from?'

'What do you mean?' asked Wilkins, climbing up the mound behind him.

'The glass,' continued Brownson, 'is not glass.'

'What is it then?'

'I'm not sure,' said Brownson, all the while speaking out of the corner of his mouth, his pipe sticking out of the other corner. 'It's like looking through ice. But obviously it's not ice. There are ice caverns in the Antarctic that are blue, because the sunlight travels through the ice.'

'But this isn't and can't be ice,' said Wilkins.

'Some sort of crystal though. Quartz? I don't know. I wonder if we can break a bit off?'

'We'd better not,' said Wilkins. 'Come inside and look. Tell me what you can see.'

They went inside.

'Not much,' muttered Brownson. 'Blasted glass, crystal, whatever it is is ruddy useless. Can't see anything. It's just translucent, no detail.'

The Sun was higher in the sky than it had been during Wilkins' previous visits of early morning and early afternoon. They could see very little through the bright windows which seemed to catch the light from above and glow, letting very little direct light in from eye level.

'Let's see this hole then,' said Brownson.

They moved over to the open hole which was just as it had been before. Brownson shone his torch down then passed it to Wilkins.

'Hold this', he said and lowered himself down. 'All right. Drop the torch down old girl,' he shouted out from below. Wilkins dropped the torch down and descended herself.

Wilkins found herself in a dry hole with a tunnel to her left and right and behind. The three short tunnels both led to small chambers, all with a large flat black stone. The chambers were fashioned from rough hewn but flat, solid stone.

'A burial chamber. Just as I thought,' said Brownson.

'But there's nothing here?' said Wilkins.

'Hello, what's this?'

Bronson's torch light had caught a glimpse of something next to one of the flat stones, something shiny. They had to lower their heads to enter the chamber. The shiny object was a torch.

'That's… my torch,' exclaimed Wilkins in a whisper.

'Eh?' said Brownson. 'You been here already old girl?' He bent down to pick up the torch but it appeared to be stuck. With a little tug it came free.

'What's this? The stone's magnetic,' said Brownson.

'How is that possible?' asked Wilkins.

Brownson took his keys from his pocket and held them next to the other two stones.

'All three are. They're 'loadstones', magnetic rocks, rich in iron.

Possibly meteorites. Interesting. But why arrange all three, cut to these neat shapes, in this pattern under the barrow?'

Even with a mystery such as this, everyday life at a small boarding school takes precedence and a few weeks past without either of them looking into the matter further or even discussing it.

'Are you in love miss?' asked one of the pupils in her class. The rest of the boys giggled.

'No, Bradshaw, I am not,' Wilkins replied.

'Mr Brownson likes you,' said another boy.

Wilkins chose to ignore this comment.

'Have you seen the ghost miss?' asked another boy.

'What ghost?' said Wilkins. 'Where?'

'The pale lady miss. We've all seen her. In the field, beyond the cottages,' said the boys.

After hearing that the school was in possession of an old ship's telescope, Wilkins decided to locate it and attempt to set it up. She'd been told to begin her search for the long ignored artefact in the attic spaces of the main house. No-one had been in the attic for some time, indicated by the fact that no-one seemed to know the whereabouts of the key to the old padlock that adorned the entrance hatch. By chance, a rusty key found in the kitchens proved to be the correct one and the hatch was opened.

Wilkins had to again rely on her torch to explore the dusty

alcoves in the loft space. There were various boxes, tea chests mostly, full of papers and books. One of them had something brass-like poking out of it. On inspection it proved to be the telescope she was looking for. It was quite a large heavy thing, over a yard long, poking out of a tea chest that contained other junk. Lifting out the heavy item she saw to her dismay that the telescope contained no lenses, except the eyepiece, but that was broken. Thinking that the lenses may be elsewhere in the chest, Wilkins began emptying the box. There were items wrapped in newspaper, dated from the end of the last century. They seemed to be ornaments of some description, made of a bluish semi translucent crystal, not unlike that of the glasshouse window material. They were a variety of sizes, all highly curved humanoid shapes, some without heads, mostly feminine looking from the shape of their bodily features. Wilkins could find no sign of any lenses in the newspaper wrappings and was about to place the items back when she found a leather bound tome at the bottom of the trunk.

The book, like the newspapers, had very brittle pages. But it was possible to flick through with care. Wilkins decided at once to borrow the book and take it down with her to study further as on the pages near the front it had, drawn in brown ink, various schematics of the tumulus and the glasshouse upon it. The dates on the drawings were 1820. That made the book one hundred and ten years old. The drawings, and presumably the writing, of which the hand was all the same, was attributed to Carolina Grimwade.

'Interesting,' said Brownson when Wilkins showed him the

book later.

'Carolina must be the Lord Grimwade's grandmother, or mother,' said Wilkins.

'There was no 'Lord' Grimwade,' said Brownson. 'Oh, Claris Grimwade was married, but her husband was never named a lord. The house and the family name was hers. Unusual that, to follow the maternal line.'

'So the glasshouse was built around 1820. What are these lines on the drawing?' said Wilkins.

There were straight lines on the drawing, coming downwards at angles onto the glasshouse roof, then angled straight downwards.

'I'm not sure, wait, look at this, it says here, 'vernal equinox'.'

'The first day of spring,' said Wilkins. 'Usually the 19th to 22nd of March.'

'That's this week,' said Brownson.

It was a morning fitting of the name 'the first day of spring'. The air still had a chill but the sky was clear and bright and birds were singing as the two made their way to the glasshouse.

'The book indicates noon, so let's see,' said Brownson. 'I've brought these, look.'

From his coat pocket he produced two rods of copper, both bent at right angles.

'What's that?' asked Wilkins.

'Dowsing rods. Just a thought I had.'

Brownson held a rod in each hand, with the longer parts pointing straight ahead in parallel. He walked around and unto the tumulus. The rods remained parallel.

'Nothing,' muttered Brownson.

They climbed the hill and entered the glasshouse. It was almost noon. The bright sun gave a blueish tinge to the translucent window panes, its crystalline structure more visible now in the bright light. The sun lit up the panes right at the top of the roof part of the structure so that they shone white. The dust in the air within the place revealed three wide beams of light angled straight down, just like in the drawing. Wilkins guessed that the beams would be aligned with the lode stones they had seen inside the hill. But there was another curious effect.

'Look!' said Brownson, pointing out through the windows. The rods he was holding pointed north. Even as he rotated his whole body, the two rods pointed that direction. Outside on the grass, where the shadow of the glasshouse should have been, was a line of flickering lights, stretching off. Excitedly, Branson left the structure to follow the line.

'The light and magnetism have created a ley line!' he said excitedly as he left.

Wilkins turned to the door to leave too when she saw, through the distorted glass, the hooded figures she had seen before, marching in a line towards the hill. She hesitated, then went to the door and stepped out. This time, the figures did not disappear. This time they came right up the hill towards her. She glanced around. Brownson was no-where to be seen.

'We find you at last,' said the nearest figure in a quiet voice. 'Come with us my lady.'

Brownson was in quite a state when the police took him away. Matron shooed the over-excited boys back to their dorms. The police had spent all day searching the area around the glasshouse as well as the fields and the cliffs and shore beyond, initially with Brownson in tow. They had spoken to the boys who had revealed their belief that Brownson had intentions towards Wilkins. Branson had discussed the visit to the glasshouse and how Wilkins had simply entered it while he was outside and when he had turned around she had vanished. He kept his theory of ley lines to himself though.

The next evening some of the boys decided to start an investigation of their own. After lights out they managed to climb out of their first floor window and using sheets tied together, lower themselves to the ground. The three bravest boys headed out to the lower field. As they approached the field with the glasshouse, they stopped dead in their tracks. The glasshouse on the hill appeared to glow a soft blue in the dim twilight. Then, from out of it stepped the figure of a woman.

'The pale lady!' said Sheddy.

'Is it...' said Murphy, then calling out, he shouted, 'Miss

Wilkins!'

The pale figure turned around to look at them and then vanished.

Brownson returned after a day. No charges had been filed.

'Perhaps she simply didn't fit in and just left us,' said Headmaster. 'Perhaps we were too hasty in relying on a female teacher.'

'What, and leave all her things behind?' said Brownson.

As Brownson returned to his rooms, a small boy called out to him.

'What is it Kevin?' asked Brownson.

'We saw her sir. The ghost. We saw her,' said the boy.

'Ghost? What ghost?' said Brownson.

'The grey lady sir. It's Miss Wilkins. She's the grey lady now.'

Council of Hex

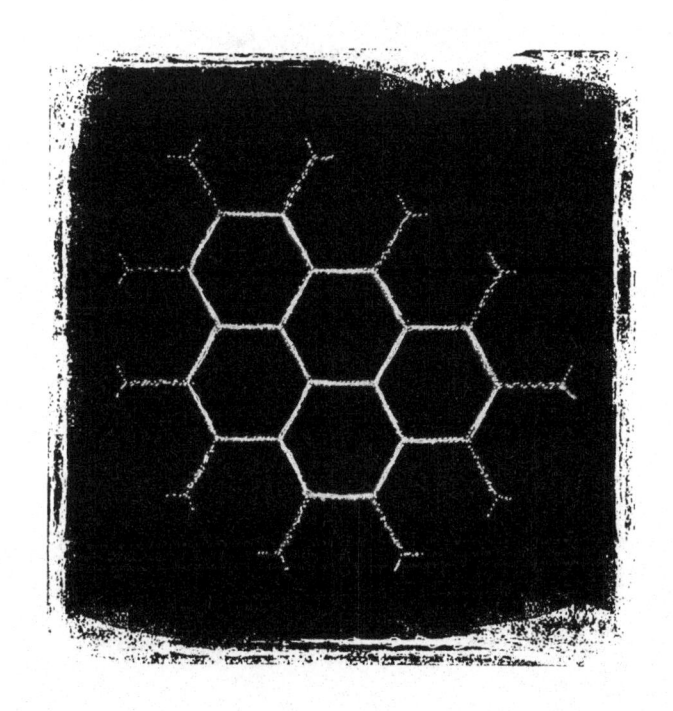

On the Shores of Lake Onyx and other weird tales

Council of Hex

I've kept all of this a secret for fifty years.

I was walking on the sea edge along the beach. It was a holiday and as an only child I was used to wandering off from wherever my parents had pitched up. As an adult, looking back on the memory, I see the men with their metal detectors far over at the cliff side of the beach. But at the time of my find, I didn't not register the irony. There were few pebbles along this part of the beach. The sea was out and there was only the soft warm golden sand. It was easy to spot the thing that had washed up, entangled in seaweed, with the next wave at my feet. Looking down I thought it was a barnacled shell and bent down to retrieve it, hoping that the creature was still inside. But this was not a shell. Something was trapped inside it, a pebble. Once that was loose, the seaweed fell away to reveal a metallic ring. It appeared to me to be made of tarnished silver with a single large ball set in it, darker than a pearl but still pearlescent. I put it in the small pocket in my bathing trunks and returned to my parents. I never spoke about it to anyone.

That night in the guesthouse I washed the ring in the sink. Even to my young eyes with no knowledge of such things, it looked very ancient. Whereas with most things, I'd always be happy to share any secret with my parents, this was different. I told no-one of the discovery. Later I convinced myself that the ring had come from the finger of a body, fallen from its grave as the sea had eroded the headland. That was the true macabre reason for the metal detectorists I had seen that day. I had to have some explanation for the provenance of the ring, as everything would change that night as I sat up in bed and idly slipped the ring onto a finger.

The room I was in, the single bed, the floral wallpaper and the antique bedside lamp, faded away. At first I could see nothing discernible. It was not like a blurred image, more like a crumpled up newspaper, a constantly changing chaotic mess that I frantically tried to grasp onto. I knew I was still seated and still in a room. A different room. An inside-out room. It was like being in an enclosed space outside the inside. As shapes formed and unformed I felt the presence of others. Light seemed to come from them. I counted five lights. They were creatures, or people, or something formless, something my brain couldn't process. It was like straining to hear music and only making out a few words and notes and not being able to recognise the tune. But they were there, of that I was certain. They were all looking at me, talking to me, with me, but not with words.

They were glad I was with them. It was a relief to them. They had been waiting. Waiting for over 10,000 years. Now, they could continue with their plan at last. For a moment, perhaps due to all this excitement, I must have pulled the ring off. I was back in the bedroom, sitting up in bed with the lamp, the floral wallpaper and the wardrobe as it had been moments before. Was it a dream, a fit, was I ill? I slipped the ring back on and I was immediately back in the circle with those others. They 'spoke' to me. They told me of their plan to save the world. My role was key. I was told I could, with their help, be given powers to influence minds. But not the mind of any individual. I would only be able to influence large groups, who were all connected, all tuned into one another already. A group that could manifest a sort of hive mind.

And that was how it started. Whenever I needed to report progress or needed further help and support, all I needed to do was put the ring on. Whenever I wore it, I was back with them, no matter where I was at the time. They were always pleased when I re-joined them. I updated them on my efforts and they seemed pleased. For many years I took their gifts and used them well.

I realise you'll find so much of this difficult to believe. But I can only laim to be directly responsible for so much. I can only give you rough guesses on specifics. You see I couldn't influence individuals, so avoiding certain wars and conflicts or changing certain political doctrines were outside my sphere. There was so much I wanted to do directly but couldn't. But I could mobilise groups, movements, focus marches and protests, empower sit-ins and strikes, spread love through a crowd at large gatherings, sow the seed of ideas such as human rights, women's liberation, vegetarianism, socialism, race, cultural and multi-faith relations, and even what became known as political correctness. I had a hand in them all. I was spreading co-operation and fair-play on a global scale. But I can take no credit of course as I can reveal no proof of any kind. You have only this account. Sometimes I wished I could have influenced leaders or governments. I asked Them, but no, the powers would not, could not, extend that way.

So why am I telling you this now? Because now I'm powerless once again. My role is at an end.

I had been rejoining the circle on and off, whenever I had something to report or needed advice. I would also hear of their particular triumphs and tribulations. Each of them was a delegate for another world. We, each member of this cosmic council, had jurisdiction and responsibility for a single dominant species on a different world. With my successes and joy in playing such a role, I had long forgotten to think about the facts surrounding my involvement. I had forgotten that I was probably not the original wearer of the ring that was located on Earth. I was in reality an imposter.

Many years had passed before they finally realised I was not one of them. I don't know how they knew or why they didn't figure it out before. I don't know what they thought I was, but as they realised, I could feel what they now knew. They realised I was not female, as they all were, and was warm blooded, as they were not. There were other differences too that were harder to feel. One of them was to do with the number six which kept coming up. Six, six, six was in my mind. It was all that was in my mind. What did that mean?

They were saddened but not angry at my deception, or rather my error. They were gracious enough that if I were to put things right and hand over the ring to its rightful bearer, my role in all this would simply come to an end. There would be no further repercussions. This was far more gracious that I can describe considering the great misdeeds and malappropriation of their gifts and time, which had led to me utterly ruining their mission for the Earth.

You see what I had been doing was just like taking money destined for a charity to stop a famine, and spending it on raising locusts that would swarm and destroy what remained of the crops. That's what I had done. But I didn't know how or to what extent at that time; only now do I understand.

I took the ring to the allotted place just before the appropriate time. I will not reveal where it was but say only that it was in an orchard. I placed the ring at the base of a tree and hid. I watched from my vantage point, hoping to get a glimpse of the creature that I was not. Who was the alien that was the rightful wearer of the ring? I did not know what to expect. The rendezvous crept ever closer. It was a warm spring day. There was blossom on the trees. She did not come. The allotted time of arrival had been and gone. Still, no-one.

The ring was still there in the grass at the base of the tree. I decided it was safe to have a closer look since nothing had approached or seemed likely to. Should I abandon the ring or take it back? Should I consult the council one more time? I looked down sadly at the ring. Maybe it was a dream? Had the whole thing been only in my mind? Was it simply a way for my brain to cope with the lack of tangible achievement in my crummy life? I had nothing to show for the last forty years. No particular job or trade, no wealth, no family, few friends. I had done nothing. Had I in fact invented all of this, as a way of justifying my total lack of ambition and progress? You must admit the story sounds much too far-fetched to possibly be true, and of course I have no evidence to show you. I no longer even have the ring.

The air was warm and full of the soft buzzing of insects as I thought all this, looking down at the ring. Then I saw it. There was something inside the ring. I bent down to look. There, sat inside was a bee. A large bee which to me looked like a queen. It was then, in that final moment that I realised the truth. I now knew who these creatures were in that council. I now realised which species I had been letting down.

The truth is that it was not a ring designed for a human finger. My very first impression of the object all those years ago was closer to the mark. It was designed for the whole body of a creature to enter. It was designed for the body of a bee.

For thousands, or probably millions of years, the Council had guided the species of the Hex through their development on five worlds. But on this one, a parasitic traitor had taken her place. I had used their powers to influence my own pathetic species at the expense of these, such noble creatures. I had done them such a disservice that their hives are on the brink of collapse, some varieties are close to extinction and every other lesser species is at risk because of it, because of my actions.

I left the bee and the ring and never returned to that place, my shameful meddling now over at last. Now that the rightful delegate has taken her place on the council, I just hope it's not too late.

The Shadow People

On the Shores of Lake Onyx and other weird tales

The Shadow People

Peter Shergold likes **Transformational Vision**

'You should look at certain walls stained with damp, or at stones of uneven colour. If you have to invent some backgrounds you will be able to see in these the likeness of divine landscapes, adorned with mountains, ruins, rocks, woods, great plains, hills and valleys in great variety; and then you again you will see there battles and strange figures in violent action, expressions of faces and clothes and an infinity of things.' – Leonardo

42 Likes 2 Comments   23 Shares

Lucy Hunter
Yesterday at 23:20
I'm not staying late in that place anymore! I saw it again last night. Same time.
You, Caroline Whicker, Tim Grimshaw, Fiona Stevenson and 4 others like this.

Caroline Whicker Take care hun! It's not worth it. They can't make you work in a place that's haunted.

Like Reply Yesterday at 23:40

Tom Singleton I haven't seen anything…yet. Did you get a photo?
Like Reply 10 hours

Lucy Hunter It's not funny. No haven't got a photo. Just seems to be watching me, out of the corner of my eye. When I look it's gone. But it's still there somewhere.
Like Reply 10 hours

Peter Shergold But that's a brand new office block isn't it? How can it be haunted? The old place maybe.
Like Reply 8 hours

Tom Singleton It's right near the Tower of London…
Like Reply 8 hours

Fiona Stevenson I've 'seen' them too. Horrible.
Like Reply 1 hour

Lucy Hunter Them???!!!
Like Reply 1 hour

What Are The Shadow People?

By gregadams • Posted in Supernatural

Just a few years ago, no-one would have believed it. No-one would have given the idea the time of day. But that was before the shadow people. The idea wasn't new to me, even as a skeptic. Prior to recent events, many thought of them as two different entities, one being the shadow figure, the misty dark figure that has no definitive form that we see it in the corners of our eye but never get a better glance. They elude us as soon as we try to look directly at them. The other is the dark robed figure, usually associated with darkness, while people are asleep. The sleeper becomes aware of a presence either approaching, crouching near or standing over them while they are in bed. Once they are aware of this presence they become overwhelmed with fear, finding themselves paralysed, not able to move nor scream and have a feeling of powerlessness. Sometimes too feeble to even pray. My feelings are they have come to feed off your fear.

Share this:
Twitter   Facebook   Google   Email
29 Votes
4 bloggers like this

Comments on "What Are The Shadow People?"

madison

I have had this experience many times in the last month. They would come and hover over my bed just watching me. When I feel myself getting paralysed and feeling frightened by it, I tell them I don't like that I can't move and rebuke them in the name of my higher power, and they immediately go and the feeling of being paralysed goes away.

janice

I think they are low vibrational entities that are associated with strong malevolent feelings and desires. A lot of folks have associated these feelings with something bad, malevolent or even demonic in nature. Remember, they can't touch us, unless we "allow" them to.

Stay in control, do not give in to fear, and put a light of protection around you and rebuke it in the name of your higher power and depending how strong this entity is will determined whether or not you'll need extra help to get rid of it.

anonymous

The only difference between genius and stupidity is that genius is limited.

jennifer

One theory is that when you're at a location where traumatic events took place, it may have left a psychic energy impression on that area if it's outdoor, or in a physical location like a home or a building or a physical item associated with that event. These beings manifest in thought forms, in other words, they are collections of negative psychic energies created by these tragic and or horrific events. But why they're suddenly more abundant, I don't know.

bill

They are inter-dimensional/transient passengers, not of this time and space. Our galaxy is filled with energy vortexes, could these entities be traveling though them? Another idea out there is that perhaps humans are traveling back in time, perhaps they cannot manifest into a solid form due to time and space, so they may look shadowy to us.

jesusislife

We are truly in the end of days! Turn back to the Lord your saviour. Only through him will you find salvation and peace.

matt

One also has to ask why shadow people appear at night and not in the day? A possible explanation could be found somewhere between metaphysics and quantum physics. It is possible that as our 3rd dimensional veil lifts, we are becoming more perceptive to beings on different dimensions or who have different vibrations. As dimensions merge and overlap, it is quite possible that many more strange, unexplainable phenomena will appear.

anonymous
Morons.

Tom Singleton
Yesterday at 19:14
It's on the news again! I thought it was totally made up!
You, Caroline Whicker, Tim Grimshaw, Fiona Stevenson and 2 others like this.

Lucy Hunter They're saying it's an optical illusion because we're spending too much time on our phones, Facebook etc etc.
Like Reply 9 hours

Caroline Whicker Like having too much blue light at bedtime?
Like Reply Yesterday at 19:40

Peter Shergold I read somewhere out our brains changing cos we're built to look at 3D things but spend too much time looking at 2D screens so maybe our brains invent stuff, out of the corner of our eyes or something?
Like Reply 8 hours

Tom Singleton But it's happening to so many people?!?
Like Reply 8 hours

Fiona Stevenson Pretty much everyone looks at screens!
Like Reply 6 hours

Peter Shergold likes **Transformational Vision**

The image at the eye has countless possible interpretations. How can you know what you have interpreted is what is actually there? How can you know that the limited field you do perceive and process is all that is actually there?

The psychic activities that lead us to infer that there, in front of us, at a certain place, there is a certain object of a certain character, are generally not conscious activities, but unconscious ones. We don't see shape and space, we see them because we have previously felt them. What we see is only coloured patches. We then associate these coloured patches with the shapes we have felt. The boy, born blind and who then later came to see, needed to see a cat whilst touching it before he could recognise it by sight alone. We have learned associations between vision and touch. The remotest of objects such as the Sun and the stars are in my eye, or rather, in my mind. Is it any wonder that you don't see them, having never touched them?
I have touched them. Now I see them.
29 Likes 4 Comments 17 Shares

Lucy Hunter

Today at 03:15

I'm deleting my account and turning off my phone. They're watching me. I want them to go away. I want this to end.

You, Caroline Whicker and Fiona Stevenson like this.

Fiona Stevenson Me too. I've got every light on in the house now. I can't sleep.

Like Reply 1 hour

Tom Singleton I'm signing off too. We've awoken something. They're saying they're in the wi-fi and there's a chance if we act now. I'm unplugging my router too just in case.

Like Reply 1 hours

Lucy Hunter Wi-fi? But we're surrounded by wi-fi!????!!!!

Like Reply 30 minutes

Peter Shergold This might be my last message. BT has switched off. Virgin still on for now. They say all mobile networks will be off within the hour.

Like Reply 20 minutes

Lucy Hunter Will that work? Will we ever be able to switch things on again?
Like Reply 10 minutes

Tom Singleton It's not looking that way. They don't know if they're coming because of the screens or the electromagnetic radiation or both. Some people have died now. They're saying heart attacks. It's too scary.
Like Reply 2 minutes

Fiona Stevenson I CAN SEE THEM. THEY'RE HERE!
Like Reply 1 minute

Peter Shergold I read it's how it's changed our brains. They're coming through us. No-one knows if this turn off is going to work. So this is it guys. Goodbye.
Like Reply Just now

On the Shores of Lake Onyx and other weird tales

---

friendface

Sorry, something went wrong.

We're working on it and we'll get it fixed as soon as we can.

Go Back

Friendface © 2020 • Help Center

Internal Server Error

The server encountered an internal error or misconfiguration and was unable to complete your request.

Please contact the server administrator to inform of the time the error occurred and of anything you might have done that may have caused the error.

More information about this error may be available in the server error log.

Service Unavailable - DNS failure

The server is temporarily unable to service your request. Please try again later.

You Are Not Connected to the Internet

This page can't be displayed because your computer is currently offline.

Crystals of Consciousness

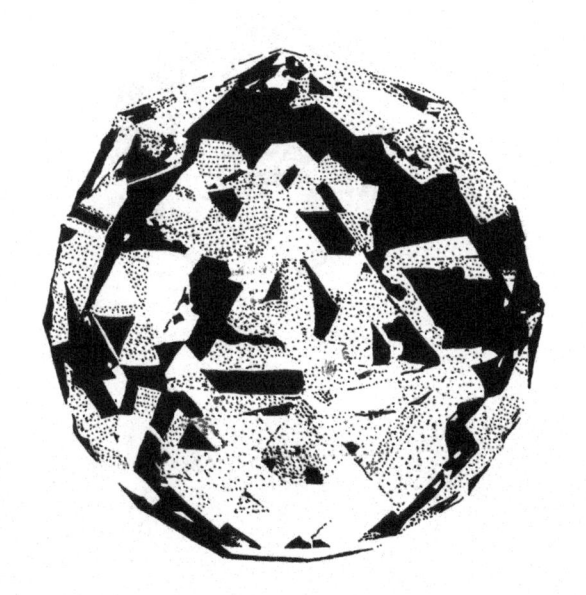

On the Shores of Lake Onyx and other weird tales

Crystals of Consciousness

I wake to sleep, and take my waking slow.
I feel my fate in what I cannot fear.
I learn by going where I have to go.

We think by feeling. What is there to know?
I hear my being dance from ear to ear.
I wake to sleep, and take my waking slow.

Of those so close beside me, which are you?
God bless the Ground! I shall walk softly there,
And learn by going where I have to go.

Light takes the Tree; but who can tell us how?
The lowly worm climbs up a winding stair;
I wake to sleep, and take my waking slow.

— Theodore Roethke

We walked through the fields, across the meadow and down through the orchard, Marianne and I. Soon there'd be some work to be done. Not much though, nothing too strenuous, just checking that the robots were preparing for the harvest. We walked hand in hand. The sky was a clear blue. I could smell figs as we entered the walled gardens. Marianne sensed my joy. I knew that wasn't her real name, but it didn't matter.

'The sky is so blue,' I said.

'Of course,' she smiled, 'if you say it is, it is.'

'I know, I know,' I said. 'What you see is totally different. It could be that you see it as what I'd call 'pink'.'

'Whatever we see, although different, feels the same. The result is the same,' she said.

She'd said this all before of course. We didn't often talk about it, and it was less on my mind these days. I looked at her, brushing her long auburn hair from her face as she picked a dandelion and blew away the seeds. We'd talked about it when we had decided to get married, I can't recall how long ago that was now, years or months, I don't know. We'd met on that first day that I arrived on the planet. It was summer that day too. She'd helped me come to terms with the aftermath of the crash, the death of the rest of the crew: Peters, Lynn and Credence. The villagers had helped bury them according to my wishes and we dismantled the remains of the shuttle there being not materials on this planet to effect repairs. Marianne was my rock, the constant that helped me cope with the fact that I could never go back, that this was now my home. There was no way to send an interstellar signal to the colonies or back to New Earth. For a while I scanned the skies at night, hoping for sight of a reconnaissance ship. She had sat with me throughout that time. The night sky was full of bight stars in their strange constellations. But no ships came. She said we must not talk about it anymore.

I'd always wanted to run a farm. Marianne said that if that's what I wanted then she would want that too. I'd lived in the hills of central Italy for the first few years of my life before moving to the city.

'A vineyard! We must have a vineyard,' I'd said to her.

'Yes, we must,' she had replied. 'Sweet red wine to toast our love!'

So we have a vineyard and the wine is so red and so sweet.

The world is there. I see it. I feel it. She reminds me that it is all real. It is real and yet its what I think it should be. Not on a conscious level. I can't desire something and then see it. What I mean is, I think, is that my mind interprets what is there, via my senses, and creates a world view of what my senses have revealed. So for me, what I see, what I feel, what I smell, taste and touch are real. But as Marianne says, that's not what is there, just what I have interpreted. She might be a purple octopus for all I know. She laughed at that suggestion once. But it's true, she might. I see her as a beautiful woman, I can see her, touch her. But my senses are being fooled. What I see is a 'translation' of what is there, she says. That goes for the wine too, the grapes the grass, the wall and the sky. We live inside our brains. Our senses fool us into thinking we're 'out there' when really we're 'in here'. Is it a feature of this world, some technology they developed, long forgotten? Has it always been like this and I just never thought about it? I wonder what she thinks I look like? What does she 'see'?

Commander Stael was worried.

'This is the right place. The ship must have come down here. So much debris in orbit. I wouldn't be surprised if they were hit,' he shouted over the rattling noise of the small ship.

'Another hit like that and we'll be joining them! We've already lost all external scanners!' shouted Pervensie.

'We daren't pull up now,' said Aktar. 'Commander, we'll have to go down whether we want to or not.'

'Agreed,' said Stael. 'Set a course, take us down.'

The small ship dived down in a desperate attempt to drop below the shell of debris that encircled the planet. Down, down, below the thin cloud cover and through the grey sky to the barren surface below. The craft was spinning out of control, the crew shouting instructions and data to each other, professional to the last. The ship plummeted to the ground, the retro thrusters firing to take the worst out of the impact. The ground was relatively soft and the small shuttle scored a long scar across its surface before coming to rest in a cloud of grey dust.

When Stael awoke he found he was the only survivor of the crash. With his helmet on he noticed he had ten hours of oxygen. The hull was breached. He located extra cylinders. That would give him two days of breathing. Possibly enough to affect repairs? He didn't know. Checking the scanner he found to his surprise the signal from Esposito's ship was still registering and very close. He had crashed in the same vicinity as the other shuttle and it was only a kilometre away. Gravity on the planet appeared Earth normal, that was of course one of the reason's this planet had been chosen for reconnaissance for a possible colonisation inspection. Stael wasted a lot of breath manually opening the hatch and using the scanner mounted on his suit's wrist he set off across the dry dirt to locate Esposito's ship.

It was a slow walk in the heavy suit but forty minutes later Stael approached the shuttle, identical to the one he had just left in every way. The hatch was open. Lying there in the doorway was the inert body of a man. His helmet was off and held in his hand. On closer inspection he saw that it was Esposito. Inside, Stael found the bodies of Peters, Lynn and Credence. They must have been killed on impact. The ship was however in better shape than his own. The oxygen store was complete. There was fuel. If he could start it, it may well be able to take off. Then he heard a sound from outside the craft. It sounded like a voice. Stael stopped and listened. He heard it again.

'Hello? Hello?' came the voice.

Puzzled, Stael turned to leave the vessel. Stood in the doorway was the figure of a man; tall, thin, pale yellow skinned with golden eyes and hair. He wore a long white garment that reached the ground.

'Come with me,' the man said.

'Who are you?' asked Stael. 'How can you be speaking my language?'

'I am Draumur,' said the figure. 'I am not speaking your words but your mind is hearing them.'

Stael ignored this for a moment. He had more important things on his mind.

'Can you help me? I need to fix this ship and get back to my mothership before I run our of air.'

'Come with me,' said Draumur.

Stael felt he didn't have many options so he would at least see where this guy was indicating, having seen nothing but wasteland on his walk to the shuttle. Perhaps this man had a ship of his own, or more people who could help? Stael followed him out of the shuttle to see the stranger walking slowing towards what looked like a plain rectangular building a few hundred meters away. Since the man was not constrained by a spacesuit, it required a greater effort from Steal to keep up. Draumur did not turn around again until he reached an opening in the large featureless structure and beckoned for Steal to enter with him inside.

The inside of the structure was as plain and white as the outside. The featureless walls, floors and ceiling were clean and bright, lit by some unseen source. To Steal it resembled an art gallery. On display on waist height slabs were transparent golfball sized crystals, spaced out and neatly arranged, sat in round indents on the slabs.

'You may take off your helmet,' said Draumur.

'Are you kidding me? There's no oxygen in here,' said Stael. He looked around. The opening they had just entered through was still open.

'Look at your readings,' said Draumur calmly.

Stael looked. Then wondered how this guy knew he had the ability to sample atmosphere external to his suit. The readings read: nitrogen 78%, oxygen 21%, argon 0.9%.

'Standard Earth levels,' said Stael. He hesitated, but decided to try. He loosened the release catches on his helmet in such a way that he could quickly re-connect them. There was no expected hiss as different pressures re-adjusted. Stael lifted the helmet and breathed the air of the room.

'You have many questions,' said Draumur.

Stael didn't really know where to start.

'Welcome to the City of Life,' said Draumur. He indicated the crystals, 'Each of these crystals contains two consciousnesses. When the craft outside crashed we were able to save one of its occupants. The others had ceased before we were able to scan. Within this crystal lives the man you called Esposito.

'What? Are you telling me that Esposito is inside that piece of glass?' said Stael.

'His consciousness is,' said Draumur.

'But he's dead,' said Stael. 'He can't be living in there.'

'The unique brain patterns that existed within the organic matrix of his brain have been duplicated and at the point of death, transported into the crystal. He is as alive now as he was before.'

This information took some processing. The stranger just stood there while Stael let it all settle in.

'But he has no body. He's trapped in there?' said Stael.

'No,' said Draumur. 'The world in his mind is as real as any world he experienced in an organic body. He will feel, see, hear, taste, smell a full rich life as he did before.'

'But he can't though can he?' said Stael. 'He can't touch anything, he doesn't exist!'

'Ah but he does, in exactly the same way he did before. The world he experienced before was also inside his head, interpreted from sensory inputs, but always inside his head,' continued Drawumu. 'He is living a fuller and richer life now, I can assure you. As are all those in this City.'

'Can I talk to him?' said Stael.

'Sadly not. Only two consciousnesses can exist in a crystal, all but these last few have two, one of our people and a guest. Once there are two, they work together to create their own universe for themselves. There can be no input from outside.'

'How many are there?' asked Stael looking around the room. There was an opening on the far side that looked like it led to another place. From the outside there had been no clue as to how big this building was.

'There are 10 billion souls here,' said Draumur.

'How many people live here, said Stael, still not really processing all this new information.

'People?' said Draumur. 'I have just said...'

'I mean real people,' said Stael. 'Like you and me. How many 'organic' people, and animals and plants, and anything else. Life. We picked up no life readings when we were in orbit. We thought this was a dead world.'

There are none,' said Draumur. 'Not now. But there is life of course.'

'No-one else? Just us? On this entire planet? How have you been surviving?'

'You misunderstand. As I said, there is no-one. There is no-one here in the form you suggest.'

'But...' said Stael. 'We are here.'

'No,' said Draumur. 'We are not.'

That last statement unnerved Stael in a way that made him feel the hairs on the back of his neck prickle. He felt threatened. There was an unseen danger here.

'I must return to my ship,' he said, making his way calmly to the door and re-positioning his helmet.

'When Esposito's ship crashed,' said Draumer, turning to follow him, 'We were able to save one soul. Your ship did not crash.'

'What do you mean?' said Stael, pausing at the doorway. 'You're saying that was a perfect landing? It killed my crew!'

'Your ship did not crash,' continued Draumer. 'It burnt up in orbit. We could not act quick enough to save more than one occupant at a time. We saved you. You were transferred to a crystal with one of us to make a perfect match of two.'

'What?' said Stael quietly, still standing by the open door. 'I crashed. I'm here. The ship is out there.'

'No, you and your ship were atomised by our deflector pods in orbit. You remain because you were saved. Your consciousness was saved in a crystal like these. We had so little time. Normally the transition is smooth. We have a chance for you to awake in a world of expectation, based on your desires. You wake up in the place you would most wish to live. With you we could only initially create a world based on what is actually here. On our planet is a building like this which houses the crystals of the City just as this. But this is not it. We too exist in a crystal, you and I. This scenario is entirely in our minds. In time, together, we will change it.'

Stael did not have much time to come to terms with this twist. The debris in orbit were mines, designed to deliberately destroy craft and harvest souls? It couldn't be true, could it? It explained a few things. No, it could not be true.

'So, you put me in this artificial reality and I create this world, everything around us?' he said. He was frustrated now, even angry.

'Yes,' said Draumer.

'So I believe you when you said I could breathe the air, I take my helmet off and low and behold, I can breath. Even though earlier I saw there was a 98% carbon dioxide reading?'

'Yes,' said Draumer.

Stael took his helmet off again and stepped back into the room.

'So if I now say, 'oh, I fancy a nice cold beer' I simply wish it, and it appears right here on this slab.'

'Yes,' said Draumer.

No beer appeared.

'Well where is it then?' shouted Stael.

'You say it, but you don't believe it,' said Draumer calmly.

'What I don't believe in it enough?' said Stael.

'Yes.' said Draumer, 'You believe that to have a nice cold beer you would need to work hard to earn money to buy one. Or, given your belief in at least part of this situation, you would need to plant barley and hops, wait for a harvest and the ferment the ingredients. After a year of effort you would have your beer. But without refrigeration you would have to drink it warm.'

Stael wasn't sure if he believed any of this at all.

'So if I have more faith, I'll have a better life? Is that it? If I accept this reality and truly believe, my powers increase?'

'Partly,' said Draumer, 'I will be here to guide you. In time it will make sense, as it did for all our people.'

'You?' said Stael.

'Each crystal contains two,' said Draumer. 'Together we will rebuild a world that will create a life of experiences worth living. You're not suited to this life, searching dead planets. Now you can live your dreams.'

'Right. So you're my 'perfect match?'. How come you're so annoying. I'm going back to my ship. I'm going to take off. I'm going to fly back to the fleet and I'm going back to New Earth,' said Stael. 'Now, are you going to let me do that? Will I find myself back here? Will I get home but find that I've dreamt it all up?'

'If you feel it's necessary to go through those motions then of course. But I will need to be with you.'

'You? Why?' said Stael, 'You can stay here with your crystals and your dreamers.'

With that he left.

Stael was glad to have left that building, that alien mausoleum. He went as fast as he could to the ship. Looking behind he could see that Draumer was not following. Then, with as much dignity as he could muster, he removed the four bodies of Esposito and his crew and placed them all in a line outside the ship. He closed the hatch. The ship came online as soon as he fired up the generator. It seemed to be in perfect order. Setting a takeoff programme he punched the controls for launch and the small craft took off, circled and accelerated upwards. From the view scanner, Commander Stael could see the featureless grey surface of the planet shrinking away. It took twenty minutes to achieve orbit. The debris that encircled the planet did not cause him any problems this time. Once into a high orbit he fired the main engines for interstellar flight back to the mothership of the fleet. In a few days he'd be able to send a signal to it, then arrange the rendezvous and then he'd be back. The first thing to do then would be to place a warning ticket on Terrelium VI. No survey would need to trouble this rotten planet again. Seven deaths! Lives lost for nothing. Stael heard a noise behind him. He whirled around. Some part of him expected to see the figure of Draumer stood there in the ship. Some part him believed what Draumer had said. But the ship was empty. He was thankfully alone. A day later he dropped out of light translational speed and sent a message to the fleet. The reply came along with coordinates and he set the guidance systems to lock on and translate to the fleet's location. Another day alone, then he'd be back.

A bleeping on the control desk woke him from sleep. The craft had dropped down into normal space. It was now time to manoeuvre manually into a docking position. It was perfect docking. His adventures had clearly diminished none of his skill. Commander Stael was met by a large contingent of pleased but sad staff. There was a lot of hugging and crying. Stael was tired. Of course he must rest and give a full report in the morning.

On waking he was met with an alert. The computers voice urged him to be ready and report to the Admiral's office for 0800. Stael was ready on time and went straight to the room. He expected to give an account of the mission, its failures that led to the deaths. He expected to have to explain the loss of one whole shuttle and its crew and the deaths of his own crew. As he entered the Admiral stood and extended his hand. There was a man sat beside the Admiral. He too stood.

'We know it's been tough for you,' said the Admiral. 'Finding the crew like that and losing your own people too. It's down to your excellent piloting skills that you managed to survive yourself. We'll place a marker on that planet so no more ships are lost due to that unusual ring of debris.'

'Thank you ma'am,' said Stael. Stael looked at the man next to the admiral. He didn't recognise him.

'A trauma like this might finish a man's service. He might be placed on indefinite leave. But not you Stael. We know you wouldn't want that,' said the Admiral. 'That's why I have a special mission for you. You'll be off normal planet scanning duties and solely assigned to this project.'

'I don't know what to say ma'am,' replied Stael.

'We have encountered a planet that could be perfect for colonisation, but there is already a developed indigenous population. Your job, as a two man team, will be to observe and monitor these peoples and see if we could at some point make formal contact.'

'Sounds just my sort of thing ma'am,' said Stael.

'Just as we thought,' said the Admiral. 'Your first degree was anthropology wasn't it?'

'Yes ma'am. You have all my career details,' said Stael.

It was just at this moment that Stael realised that she should not have all his details. His career yes, but he had not yet filed any report on the disastrous mission. All they should know is that the crew and a shuttle have been lost, no details. This all seemed so perfectly normal and yet horrendously strange.

'Let me introduce to your scientific advisor who will accompany you on the mission.' said the Admiral indicating the man stood next to her. 'This is Professor Draumer.'

Draumer extended a hand.

'Nice to see you again Commander Stael,' said Draumer.

> Great Nature has another thing to do
> To you and me, so take the lively air,
> And, lovely, learn by going where to go.
>
> This shaking keeps me steady. I should know.
> What falls away is always. And is near.
> I wake to sleep, and take my waking slow.
> I learn by going where I have to go.

— The Waking by Theodore Roethke, 1953

Silver Light

On the Shores of Lake Onyx and other weird tales

Silver Light

I know, I know, few indulge in authentic film photography these days. The majority wouldn't even know what it was. I have had this problem with my students. I'd been trying to explain the processes of light, of chemical image 'development', of negatives, etcetera etcetera only to find they had no knowledge at all of any these concepts. I couldn't even use them as analogy or metaphor in my teaching, these millennials only being familiar with the indefinable magic of the push-button digital selfie. So I took great delight in setting up a blackout dark room in my lab, equipped with the relevant chemicals from the chemistry lab next door, film and an antique enlarger. I was ready.

To make the process truly authentic I had shunned my own Canon film SLR from the mid-nineties and searched for something more fitting. I found the perfect apparatus by chance. By the edge of the Christmas market in town, amongst the artisan foods, cottage crafts and seasonal fayre, some sort of local tinker had set up a stall, purporting to be an antique dealer. His table beheld a shocking array of broken junk, many uninteresting brass items, 1980's electronics and 78 records. Amongst all this, overlooked and almost hidden, was a folding plate camera. I couldn't believe it. I was almost ashamed to ask him how much he wanted, knowing in advance that I had spotted a most amazing bargain.

It was a Victorian wet and dry plate stereo tailboard camera in excellent condition. I need not tell you that such an apparatus is extremely rare. It was housed in very high quality mahogany with the original French varnish intact. The burgundy leather bellows were in excellent condition. It was complete with a septum and two lens-boars with very rare stereo lenses: Ross London 8,5 x 6,5 Rapid Symmetrical. An ivory plaque underneath read: Murray & Heath, 69 Jermyn St, London. Unusually, the lenses and body were silver plated. I had never seen that before, adding to its value and uniqueness.

It felt a little like theft to hand over five quid for something I knew was worth around five to seven thousand pounds. I was conscious my excitement and greed was visible as I handed over the measly amount for the treasure.

When you are so used to the instantaneous gratification of digital photography, it is a shock to the system to have to return to the waiting game of film. I felt almost blind, pointing the camera at this scene or that, having to calculate the focal length manually, not really knowing the light metering, guessing an aperture and finding the shutter mechanism unreliable. Then I had to go through the entire dark room rigmarole before I would discover if my efforts were worthy or in vain. The first three attempts proved to be the latter. Spoilt plates, blurred images or just too dark resulted in boring silvery blurred nothingness on the film. I couldn't tell if it was light leakage into the camera or my dark room that was spoiling it or whether I was just plain incompetent. The fifth attempt was, by accident, all together different and the results were as unnerving as they were inexplicable.

I had often indulged in low-light digital photography. Leaving the shutter open for a prolonged time allows more photons of long wavelengths from the very low intensity of early evening light to create an eerie and haunting outside scene. Setting the smallest aperture restricts the light entering the lens further but gives a greater depth of field leading to sharper images. To compensate for this reduced light one has to use a high ISO setting (ISO being the sensitivity of the sensor to light). With film, the ISO is set in the chemical composition of the film one decides to use. With the film stock suitable for the Murray & Heath, especially with it being a stereoscopic camera, I was limited to a small choice of ISO, the most sensitive being ISO200. I fancied trying my hand at a series of twilight shots. The weather was good, a cold and fresh late December evening. But the bonus, that I felt would compensate for the film's poor sensitivity was that it was a full Moon that night.

I set the camera on a tripod and looked for a suitable setting. Looking east down the lane from the cottage looked the most promising with the still visible glow from the sunset in the west partially illuminating a row of trees, silhouetted against the horizon. The Moon was overhead, staring down. I took a number of photos with a variety of settings to increase the chance of at least one good shot. I had, I counted back in the lab, thirteen shots. Time was against me the next day and I had only time to attempt the processing of ten of them. Disappointingly, they proved to be as useless as my previous attempts. I returned to process the last three later that evening, quietly confident that the settings on these, learning what I had done from previous experiments, would be good enough to form credible photographs.

Before I go on I must explain the basics of stereo photography. Stereo or 3D photography dates from the same year as mono or traditional photography, 1839. The method is simple enough. The camera has two lenses instead of one and captures two images, side by side, on the same photographic plate. The prints are developed and viewed through a simple stereo viewer (usually two lenses mounted on a piece of vertical card) which allows the right eye to see the right image and the left, the left image. The brain then combines the two images just as it does ordinarily with the slightly different view each eye has. The result is that the photograph appears to jump out of the flat surface. Modern techniques of using false colour, polarising glasses or lenticular plastic all achieve the same effect in the same way.

I was rinsing the last three pieces of film that would form my negatives in the fixer fluid when I noticed what I'd done - or not done. The blinds over the lab windows were up. I had gone through the entire developing process, a process that should have been done in total darkness, with the blinds up and stray light from outside streaming in. It was of course night, and out here in the countryside on the edge of the moor it got pretty dark at night. But that night was still a full Moon. The silver lunar light had been shining in throughout the developing of these last three images. Of course, I had used the red lamp which had allowed me to see what I was doing without fogging the film, and that had made me unaware that the moonlight had been present.

The fixer chemical is the final stage which stabilises the image, removing the unexposed silver halide remaining on the photographic film leaving behind the reduced metallic silver that forms the image. But now, the silver halide would have all been exposed to the light of the Moon, making the entire piece of film black and any prints made from it, totally useless.

But that hadn't happened. There were images. Strange looking images. On all three pieces of film. It's hard to make out what you're looking at on a negative, especially when it's quite small (it had to be to fit two stereo images side-by-side). So I went straight to setting up the enlarger to make a positive print of the final shot. That part of the process went quickly and smoothy. As I swilled the paper in the developer, then the fixer and then water to rinse it, I saw the image taking form. I didn't wait for the paper to dry, instead I mounted it under the stereo viewer, shone a lamp down on it and looked through.

The black and white image showed the silhouetted trees, black against the dark grey sky, just as expected. But there, in the foreground were five distorted, amorphous humanoid forms. All glowing silver, with outstretched arms and demented faces with what looked like uneven sunken dark eyes. Because I was looking at a three-dimensional image it was clear that the figures were but a few metres away, in a line, as if walking towards me.

I stepped back from the viewer and saw that the blinds on the windows were still up. Outside, the Moon shone down on the lane. I looked out. The trees were silhouetted against the dark grey sky. The lane was dark and empty. I backed away from the window. Had I imagined it? I returned to the stereo viewer and looked down once more.

There were the silhouetted trees, black against the dark grey sky, as before. And to my horror, the hideous figures were there, but this time only three. But they were not in the middle distance as before, but somehow closer, much closer than before, right up close in fact, almost on top of me, almost touching me, reaching out to me. As I looked, I was aware the two missing figures must be behind me, the figures had encircled me.

I jumped back from the viewer and switched on all the main lab lighting. I closed the window blinds as fast as I could, desperately trying not to look outside as the Moon's silvery light shone down. I went to grab the three negatives and the single print and throw them away. But looking at them again, both the three film negatives and the one print I had developed showed nothing but a square of a silvery blur.

The next day I thought about selling the camera or giving it to a charity. Somehow I felt that would be wrong. At around noon, the brightest time of day I could hope for, I went for a long, long walk. Somewhere on a distant country lane, I left the camera on a dry stone wall and walked back quickly before it got dark.

Two Heads

On the Shores of Lake Onyx and other weird tales

Two Heads

'I agreed to the drink, thank you, but I've no intention of getting involved with this and I don't even know why you think my opinion counts,' Mel took a sip from her pint of cider.

'Doctor Turner, come on, you're not only one of Oxford's most highly regarded researchers but you have a reputation for, how shall we say it, the unusual.'

Mel didn't really know who these Americans were. It had been one of her students who has suggested she agree, against her better judgment, to a meeting. She was only convinced when the meeting was arranged to take place in The Eagle and Child pub.

'This is, at best, psychology, or biology. I'm a physicist. This is not my area,' she stated flatly.

'But it is. Let me explain,' said Marsden, who, she thought, may or may not be the senior of the two, but was certainly the most vocal. 'It is computer science. You can admit that. That's the first reason why we need you. We want to convince you so that with your reputation we can get support. You can get time on the university's supercomputer. You can help us.'

'You still have to pay, whoever accesses the system. You can book it in loads of ways through your own university. So again, why me?' she asked.

'We all know you have an interest in artificial intelligence, this project is a new approach. You're on record as saying you felt true AI was possible, but needed a new kind of thinking for it to work. We believe we've found that route and we want to convince you.'

'But you've been telling me about research with human brains. I'm sorry gentlemen but you can't claim to have made a breakthrough in AI by using an actual human mind. That's not AI. That's… well, weird.'

'Exactly! 'Unorthodox, risky and liable to bring the institution into disrepute', isn't that how the committee described you after your, what was it called, your quasar time viewer?' there was an edge in his voice, almost threatening.

'I don't know what you mean,' Mel lied, 'You must be mistaken.'

'Don't take me for a fool Doctor Turner. It may be Oxford's secret, but we know all about it. That project failed we know, but your innovative thinking, open mind and approach caught our attention. We'd like you to advise on our latest developments.'

Marsden took a sip from his scotch, 'All this time, all these years, all the world's AI researchers have been trying to create a single neural net, a singular artificial intelligence and we've all got it wrong all these years. It's not the neural net that's important, it's the fact that there are two of them and it's the interplay between them that creates the ephemeral concept of 'consciousness'. You and I are not individuals, but are beings floating between two brains, our own two brains.'

'I've heard of the bicameral mind, if that's what you're thinking about,' said Mel.

'I read your paper on cosmology,' said Marsden. 'You said, did you not, that the universe itself, on the largest of scales, and I quote, 'resembles that of a gigantic neural net'.'

'That was a long time ago. I was being poetic. The universe doesn't think,' said Mel

'You said yourself, the Earth's information superhighway, the connectedness of every computer device, must be like a neural net,' continued Marsden. 'You said it, but you were wrong. It was only half. Now we know. Now we can connect it up to its other hemisphere.'

'What other hemisphere?' asked Mel.

'A source of chaos, of randomness, where a trillion trillion changes may and can happen,' said Marsden.

'A source of chaotic movement of particles?'

'Yes.'

'What, like a nice cup of hot tea?' said Mel indignantly.

'No, and yes, better than that,' continued Marsden. 'The Earth's weather system. We're connection the entire internet as the left hemisphere to the right of the planets atmospheric particle motion. But we're getting ahead of ourselves. Let me tell you about the first experiment.'

A second round of drinks appeared and Marsden continued.

'Many years ago we carried out a series of human experiments.

How this all began was totally by chance. In the first case, our patient suffered damage to the skull in an accident, the corpus callosum, that the joins the two hemispheres together had been cut. There was damage to the right hemisphere and severe haemorrhaging. We ending up deciding to remove that half of the brain. At the same time we had another case with a fatal head trauma. That body had been left to science so we decided to use it to store the other person's right hemisphere within it, to try a brain transplant into our donor body.'

'That's sick,' said Mel. 'What do you think you were doing?' She picked up on the depersonalised language that Marsden was using when talking about real people.

'We were doing the right thing for the first patient. But we weren't prepared for what happened. That patient made full recovery and is now fully alive and fully aware.'

'But with half a brain? What does he do now, work for the government?' said Mel.

'Come now, Doctor Turner. What happened next was far more momentous. The donor body made a full recovery too.'

'What?' said Mel.

'We were wrong about the right hemisphere. It too made a recovery and another 'Mr Jones' walks the Earth. When I say 'full recovery', I mean both people are well. They are not quite fully functioning. Mr 'Right' Jones can't talk. The language functions are controlled in the left hemisphere which he doesn't have. Oh, his half can imagine and see the big picture, he can gesture etc. But not talk.

Mr 'Left' Jones can't make any decisions. He can only do what he's told to do other than what is instinctive.'

'Are you hinting at the fact that the two men are the same one man, just in separate bodies?' said Mel, 'and that they…'

'They have two brains but share one mind. In other words, neither of them are conscious. We have two unconscious men.'

This was just about enough for Mel. She quickly made her excuses and left.

It was about six months later, long after she had forgotten all about the brain transplant nonsense that she was reminded of Marsden again. He had obviously got to one of her contacts and persuaded him to get her back in touch.

'It's just so weird Mel, you've got to see this loon,' said Goose.

Against her better judgement, Mel found herself in a live linkup via Skype to Marsden's lab in the US.

'Can there be a more momentous moment than this? Can there be such a more important switch than this?' said Marsden.

'It just looks like a £2 switch from Maplins,' whispered Goose to Mel.

'Tell us again doctor what this is all about. What's actually in those tanks?' asked Mel.

'My discoveries into the two brains needed for full consciousness, that was the missing piece of the puzzle to develop true AI,' said Marsden.

'We know that bit,' said Mel. She still wasn't cutting Marsden any slack.

'This unit,' said Marsden, pointing to one of the large perspex cubes, about the size of a large suitcase, filled with a translucent turquoise liquid and surrounded by insulating material, pipes and wires, 'is the neural net. An artificial brain. The most advanced ever made. Self-learning and extremely fast. This hemisphere is the processor. And this,' he pointed to another on the same desk, 'is another, almost identical except that this one has access to everything, the sum total of human knowledge, as well as live data on the Earth's weather and other chaotic systems. When I flick this switch, the two will connect and it will, we believe, create a living consciousness. A real mind created out of all human recorded knowledge, from ancient books to news websites, from every blog written to every email or tweet sent. What kind of mind will rise form that? We are the sum of our memories. What if your memories were all that has been posted online over the past thirty years? What sort of individual would you be? What would you believe? Who would you be? What would you want to do? We are about to find out!'

There were various assistants mingling about in lab coats, looking at the numerous screens which were everywhere.

'It's a bit of a spectacle this isn't it?' whispered Mel to Goose.

Marsden pressed the switch. Data streamed in. They heard it as sound, a loud, sawlike repeating pulse. They had it on screen as a flashing pulsating fractal of colour. They had it as a constant steam of ones and zeros. Every interface gave a pattern.

'It's speaking! It's speaking to us!' said Marsden in excitement. 'Just think what we've done! An artificial intelligence that comes out from the sum of all human knowledge!'

'So what is it saying?' asked Goose.

There were words on one of the screens, the same words repeated over and over again, 'ho I am who I am who I am who I am who I am…'

'Look!' said Marsden, "Who I am' over and over again. There, you see, an identity, and individual! We've done it! It's wondering who it is! It's asking that fundamental question every sentient being has asked from time immemorial: who am I?'

'Doctor Marsden, er, look, no, no, it's not. Look,' said Mel trying to catch Marsden's attention via her screen. 'There's a clear break, a pause. It's not saying 'Who I am', it's saying, 'I am who I am'. It's an assertion of identity.'

'I am who I am? Now where have we heard that before?' said Goose.

'I'm no theologian, but you know that it's from Genesis chapter two,' replied Mel.

'What's that?' said Marsden, not listening properly.

'This 'being' of yours is very clear who or what it is,' continued Mel, "I am who I am'? The sum total of human experience, tempered by the patterns of nature? It's claiming to be Yahweh, Jehovah. Congratulations gentlemen, you've just created God.'

After that, Mel managed to avoid Marsden and his creation for about six months. Then he got in tough once again by Skype.

'Doctor Turner. We really need you indulgence this time, your support and help. We have perfected our system. We've further developed and tested our new brain. We've selectively cleared some of its memory so that it can access data as a human would rather than as an omnipotent being would. Here is the brain,' Marsden gestured to the same large tanks behind him. 'Along with these supercooled tanks, the supporting supercomputers and electronics, the system cannot be moved, otherwise I'd bring it to you. But I have found a way for you to experience it first hand.'

'What do you mean?' asked Mel.

'Since it's obviously impossible to house this brain in a mobile form, we've developed a way to have a mobile body unit with a receiver and transmiter the brain signals to it. So the body can move and walk around, controlled by the brain that remains here at our facility.'

'I see. Surely the body with the receiver needs to be within range of the signal,' said Mel.

'It's a GPS signal, so as long as there's no shielding, the signal can be received and our body can move some considerable distance.'

'How far?' asked Mel.

'Well, we can't receive a signal on an aircraft so our body has to travel by ship. And that's exactly what we've done. We've sent our mobile AI unit to see you. I hope that you'll welcome a very unique visitor sometime tomorrow,' said Marsden.

The next day, Mel was in her small office in the department. Sat at another desk was her research assistant drinking tea. Unusually for him, he was wearing a suit.

'What time is the funeral?' asked Mel.

'2.30,' said Goose. 'But I want to hang on as long as I can here in case this thing turns up.'

They didn't have to wait long. At ten o'clock there was a knock at the door. Mel opened it. A woman walked in.

'You must be Doctor Turner. I've come from Doctor Marsden. You should be expecting me. I'm Cally,' said the woman in a gentle American accent.

'Cally who?' said Mel.

'Just Cally.'

Goose put his tea down and got to his feet, dipping his tie in the tea in the process. The woman entered the room, followed by two serious faced men in suits who didn't feel the need to introduce themselves.

'Hi, I'm, well, people call me the Goose,' he said, offering his hand to the newcomer. She ignored him.

'We were expecting you to bring something for us to see. Marsden said he was sending us his AI robot,' said Mel.

'That's correct Doctor,' said Cally as she walked up to the spare chair and sat down.

The two dark suited men just stood inside the room near the doorway.

'Is it here?' asked Goose.

'It is,' replied Cally. 'It is me.'

'What do you mean?' asked Mel.

'This body belonged to a woman who died of a brain tumour, her brain was completely removed and the remote reviewer system was wired into the skull and connected up to the nervous system of this body,' said Cally.

'Ridiculous,' said Mel.

'So, let me get this straight,' said Goose. 'Your brain is in Marsden's lab in the US, with it's instructions being beamed into your body here?'

'That's right. Two heads are better than one. I am both here and in the US. Although since I have no senses back in the lab, I feel only that I am here. I can sense this room with nine senses.'

'So if you died here, or rather, if this body that's here was destroyed, you'll still be 'alive' so to speak?' said Goose.

'Correct,' said Cally with a continuous coolness, almost to the point of being smug. 'I would simply need a new body with a new receiver and I would again 'feel' alive. Before I was set up in this body I could think, but not feel. I do not wish to go back to that state although I accept that one day that time will come and I hope that it will be only as a temporary situation.'

This was all getting too weird for Mel, although Goose seemed to be getting into it.

'Ok, let's assume for a moment that what you say is true, although I refuse to simply accept it. Why are you here?' asked Mel. 'I mean, what is this really all about?'

'Doctor Marsden, as I'm sure you're aware, is not respected in the scientific community,' said Cally. 'Yet he knows his groundbreaking work has extreme value and importance. This discovery is so important that it needs to be published. On his own, Doctor Marsden cannot publish. If you were to publish, either jointly with Marsden, or even on your own but citing his name in the journal, he'll be able to re-build his reputation.'

'I see,' said Mel. It was of course a ridiculous plan. So ridiculous in fact that it made that reason sound believable.

'Here is a complete set of Doctor Marsden's notes so far,' said Cally, as one of the men handed her something which Cally handed to Mel. It was a USB stick.

'I'd like to believe your story,' said Mel. 'But I'm sure you realise that we'll have to run some tests with you to back up your claims. You do realise that what you're saying sounds impossible.'

'Improbable yes, impossible no,' said Cally.

'Well since you are here, we might as well give you a tour,' said Mel.

'Thank you. But I must not leave this facility or my arranged hotel until Doctor Marsden arrives,' said Cally. 'I need to make sure that wherever I go, my receiver can still pick up the GPS signal from my brain. I can connect to internal wi-fi as a backup if the building is too heavily shielded.'

Goose had to go off to the funeral. A tour was organised and went along uneventfully. Cally asked lots of dull questions. All the time Mel was trying to think of some way to test her. She was convinced something was amiss and that she was being played. They came to a staircase.

'Our robotics devision, small though it is, is downstairs. In the basement,' said Mel, pausing in the stairwell.

'Does it maintain internet access incase the concrete of the building shields my signal?' asked Cally.

'Of course,' said Mel.

They descended the stairs and entered a brightly lit and well equipped electronics laboratory. Cally started to blink, and then sway as she entered. The researchers in the room came over just as she collapsed to the floor.

'What's happened?' one of them asked.

'Help me get her upstairs,' said Mel. They all helped to get her to her feet and back upstairs.

When Cally was back on the ground floor, he eyes opened and she came round.

'Are you ok? What happened?' asked Mel.

'There was no signal,' said Cally.

'So sorry about that. Let me take you to a place to recover,' said Mel.

'We have rooms arranged,' said one of the two men. 'We will call you later and return at 9am.'

With that, the three of them left.

Later, Goose was back, dressed as normal in loose fitting scruffy jeans and a faded rock tee-shirt. Mel had filled him in on the afternoon's events.

'Did you know the room didn't have wi-fi or wasn't able to pick up a signal?' asked Goose.

'Well, yes, I did. She asked me if they still had internet down there. I said they did, and they do, it's just not via wi-fi, they use the ethernet cable down there so I didn't actually lie,' said Mel.

'So does that prove she's telling the truth?' asked Goose.

'No. She faked it. I'm sure of it. I doubted for a while, but somehow she knew. I think it was all faked to try to convince us. Marsden must have got plans of the building or something so she knew where to pretend to faint,' said Mel.

'I don't know what's more ridiculous,' said Goose. 'Someone pretending be a robot or her story actually being true.'

'Listen, how would you pretend to be a robot?' said Mel.

'Don't you mean, how would you pretend to be human?' said Goose.

'No, it's more like, how would you be a human, pretending to be a robot who's pretending to be a human?' said Mel. 'There must be something that she does that'll give her away.' Mel paused to think,

'Does she know too much?'

'What do you mean?' asked Goose.

'If you had only information, not experiences, what wouldn't you know?' said Mel.

'Oh, you mean sort of general knowledge and facts. She could look that up so she'd know everything?' said Goose.

'No, the opposite. Marsden said her memory had been limited to make her more realistic. Who wants to interact with a know-all? No, I mean, does this actor 'Cally' know more about people and relationships, about love, about being a woman, about growing up as a child, or something, than she would not know if her stupid story were true. There are nuances that you can't just Google if you really were a brain in a lab born yesterday.'

'I see. But she could easily feign ignorance. You know, pretend she wishes she went to school or whatever. We could ask if she believes in God or something?' said Goose.

'No, that's either a yes or no. There's no big reveal there,' said Mel. 'We need to catch her out with something that she doesn't realise is intrinsically human and something that you can't learn about, you're not taught, you just do it from experience without thinking. It's the opposite of the Turing Test.'

'Like what?' said Goose.

'I don't know do I? That's what I'm trying to get us to think of,' said Mel, getting infuriated at the ridiculousness of the situation. Then it hit her.

'Your tie!' exclaimed Mel.

'What?' said Goose.

'When your tie dipped embarrassingly in your tea. She didn't laugh, she didn't smile, she smirked. She knew it was funny and withheld it. A robot wouldn't know that, or how to do that, or why to do that. A robot would have done nothing, or something obviously noticeable. Not something so subtle that I've only just realised it now. Humour can't be learnt!'

'So a robot doesn't know what's funny or what's not. Like the programme commissioner of BBC Three,' said Goose. 'Let's lay a trap to test her. How about taking her to some stand up?'

'Too easy for her to say that she's copying the responses of those around her,' said Mel.

'How about we get a comedian in here? Some slap stick actor could come in and drop stuff. Very funny. I've seen it done. He picks up all these bits of wood and always drops one and as he tries to pick it up he drops a different one. It's very funny. But she wouldn't know that and would either laugh or not laugh and then we'd know.'

'We'd know what exactly?' said Mel.

They fell silent for a while. Then Mel spoke up again.

'You could chat her up,' she said.

'You're asking me? Are you serious?' said Goose. 'Why do you think I'd know how to do that? I can only talk to you properly because you're my boss. And what if I 'got lucky' and ended up sleeping with a cadaver with a radio in its skull? No, you can try it. Maybe she's a lesbian?'

'There's no point. Again, it proves nothing,' said Mel. 'Why don't we stick to what we're best at.'

'Physics,' said Goose. 'I'll build a jamming device. She'll never know it's on and won't be able to fake a swoon.'

'Can you do it by the morning?' said Mel.

'Depend on it,' said Goose.

They knew that Cally and her two goons would be back at 9am and that Marsden would be joining them soon after. The trap was set.

'Ok, they're on their way up. Let's get them a coffee first,' said Mel.

'It's timed to start jamming in fifteen minutes. We won't be near any equipment so they'll not twig,' said Goose.

The door opened and Cally and her men entered.

'Did you have a good evening?' said Mel.

'It was ok,' replied Cally.

At that moment a loud electronic siren deafened their ears.

'Fire alarm,' shouted Mel over the noise. 'We'll congregate in the car park.'

They made their way to the stairs. The building was not packed, people were not running so Mel didn't know quite how it happened. It must have been just a terrible accident. Afterwards Mel had seen that the stiletto heel on one of Cally's shoes had broken off. Her ankle had twisted and she had fallen backwards down the stairs. Not a great distance, but the back of her head hit the edge of a step. They all rushed up to her, lying there, bleeding and motionless.

'She's unconscious,' said Mel.

The two security men made a call. The department receptionist called 999. A first responder arrived very quickly. Cally was stretchered into the car and driven away along with the two silent men. Around this time the jammer would have switched on, but she was gone and probably out of range.

Over the next few hours, Mel tried to get information on what was going on but she couldn't get close. Cally hadn't been taken to the John Radcliffe hospital, that was certain. A real ambulance had turned up minutes after the car had taken her away. Marsden was said to have been arriving in Oxford but he hadn't so far. Mel reluctantly called Marsden's office. An administrator had answered and told her that Marsden had certainly not left for England and that he had been arrested for fraud. His experiments were to be closed down. Mel's phone rang. It was reception. They had just had a strange call from someone with an American accent saying that Cally had sadly died.

Mel didn't know quite what to think. Had she been a robot? Was she an actor? Was it all an elaborate hoax? If so, what for? If Cally was a real woman playing the part, she could be dead now, or was the announcement of death another ruse? If she had been the robot then, like Cally had said, she'd still be alive. Mel felt slightly guilty for thinking that Cally had been a real woman. It would be better if she had been a robot. She turned to Goose.

'You know what proves you and I are human?'

'No, what?' said Goose.

'The fact that we're so uncertain and we don't know anything,' said Mel.

'You might be right,' said Goose.

The Curse of Baphomet

On the Shores of Lake Onyx and other weird tales

The Curse of Baphomet

"The flame of intelligence shining between his horns is the magic light of the universal balance, the image of the soul elevated above matter, as the flame, whilst being tied to matter, shines above it."

– Eliphas Levi, *Transcendental Magic: Its Doctrine and Ritual.*

Part I: Early experiments

The name of Joseph Steinberg was first brought to the public's attention, or rather the attention of the local news of the county of Oxfordshire, during the summer of 1999. The police had been called to obscure farmland off the beaten track on the edge of a Cotswold village to a disturbance in and around an ancient disused church. The small church, no more than a chapel, was in the grounds of a manor farm, once part of the Blenheim estate, accessible via a public bridleway. It had been disused for close to a century with only the rotten wooden slats on its small square bell tower visible above the overgrown ash trees and brambles that hid almost all other trace of its existence. The disturbance that the police were alerted to was triggered by the shouting of around twenty angry villagers, many of them workers on the farm, armed with various sharp agricultural implements and carrying torches from the main road and down the mile long bridleway to the overgrown copse that hid the old church.

The group had been assembled in haste based on the observations of a local man Charles Smith, out for an early evening walk, who came upon unnatural noises that had frightened his dog. On approaching the copse, Smith had seen what he described as 'eerie coloured lights' and chanting accompanied by 'inhuman wails'.

Apparently, it became the final straw of strange rumours surrounding the church as he reported it in the nearest pub an hour later and a group of vigilantes were quickly assembled by nightfall.

The noise of the drunken rabble, trying to force their way through the wall of brambles, clearly alerted whoever was inside the church, as by the time the company had broken down the main church door, which had clearly been boarded up for a very long time, all but one had fled. One youth had tripped over the threshold of the north door through which the group had made their entrance and swift exit. Oliver Sewell was dragged outside and the velvet robes he wore ripped from him. It was lucky for him that it was at that moment that two police squad cars arrived on the scene.

After holding Sewell in one car, and attempting to calm the mob down and slowly persuade them to return home, the police finally investigated what had been going on in the 12th century building. The church had been stripped of pews and other furniture decades ago. What rubbish that remained had been moved to one end, leaving the nave area clear. Around the walls were lit candles made of black wax. On the stone floor was marked a large five pointed star, in the centre of which were the ashes from a small fire which gave off a metallic smell. Jars containing metallic powders lay scattered on the floor. Why it took so long for the officers to see it, they couldn't later recall, but all four of those present saw the thing at once as they turned their attention and torches to the altar shrine end of the nave. There, apparently stood on two hairy cloven feet was, by the officers testimony, the devil himself.

They all staggered backwards at the sight of this apparition. It was Carol Temple, the only WPC present, who realised that the figure was not only corporeal, but a mismatch of various animals, bits and pieces. The trunk and legs were from a black ram, the bare torso and arms from some female shop mannequin with bare breasts. The grotesque apparition had the head of a goat with a lit flaming torch between its large horns and the sign of the pentagram painted on its forehead. The hideous creature had large feathered wings attached to its back.

The nature of the vile ceremony was obvious to everyone who read the account in the *Oxford Mail* the following week. The band of despicable Satanists were clearly trying to manifest some ancient evil in that holy place. Sewell had been questioned at length, although knew very little, having turned out to be a lowly follower within the blasphemous cult, the leader of which was identified to be one

Joseph Steinberg.

It was around this time that there had also been reports of disturbed graves in two of the villages around. Someone had attempted random exhumations but had been disturbed by locals or security lights and had given up. The police took great delight in bringing in Steinberg, hoping to pin both these and the church incident (which would be charges of breaking and entering, causing affray, disturbance of the peace along with anything else they could think of).

Steinberg turned out to be a fascination and a disappointment. The police could not place him anywhere near any of the events. He had clearly been the ringleader of the occult group but hadn't been present or authorised that particular ceremony. The police did pull in two further suspects and charged them but the public's imagination was captured by the story surrounding Steinberg's arrest and the macabre findings at his house.

The police had traced Steinberg to his bleak unassuming cottage, no more than a small farmhouse and adjoining barn. Downstairs was one large room which looked like some kind of alchemist's laboratory. There was a mixture of old and new: large leather bound tomes of ancient magick and electrical equipment, computers as well as flasks of strange liquids. It was photos of this magician's treasure trove that earned Steinberg the epitaph of 'the Real Harry Potter' after the popular new book of the same name. The remains from various animal sacrifices were kept out of the paper to preserve the more acceptable wizardry of the story rather than the unpalatable darker truth.

Steinberg had described the local occult group (that he had virtually founded) as infantile fantasists fixated on religionism and cliched modernist occult paraphernalia. Every statement he made about anyone placed himself in a higher position and as a higher authority above the fools that he had disappointingly expected more from. Even the police he viewed with bored disdain, confident in his innocence and annoyed that his real plans, whatever they were, had been disrupted. As usual, public interest lasted only for the lifetime of the paper the story was printed in and within a couple of weeks focus had moved on to the city's plans for the millennium and Steinberg and his eccentricities were forgotten. It was much later, after the main incident, when other interested parties tried to piece together a profile of who he was and where he came from when a few more scant details emerged.

As a youth, in the nineteen-eighties, people vaguely remembered a quiet, solitary Steinberg having the strange appearance of a pale white face, dark hair, black clothes and a long dark jacket always worn, even in summer. His contemporaries found him a little too eccentric even for their goth subculture, having the accoutrements of that teen movement without any effort on his part as opposed to the fancy dress look of the standard goth.

Oxford described him as an unexceptional student in the early 1990s when he read physical sciences and theology. His few pale faced girlfriends of the era all turned out to live normal sedentary lives, having little or no interest in any memory of him. Once his parents died, he became even more solitary, even those who shared a bedsit with him never really spoke or even saw him with any regularity. He was known to frequent a number of obscure university societies including one that claimed to be based on the Hermetic traditions but he soon lost interest when he discovered they were more intent on hedonism than the occult.

One girl had later reported in some interview that she remembered him becoming fearful of the Sun, that it burnt his face and skin and that he had covered his windows in grease proof paper to diffuse the light before installing black-out blinds and red bulbs in the light fittings. She had put that down, and the collection of chemicals in his room, to his interest in photography as the room was decorated with lines of string with pegged photographic paper. Although she had never seem him take any photos or even remembered him even having a camera. She had said that the pictures she saw were blurred and uninteresting, of half formed figures in shadows.

Soon after leaving university he seemed to disappear, there was no record of any vocation and no institution that had signed him up for further study of which he would have been more than capable. Some say he left the UK to finalise his parents' interests in Canada.

In any event, when he returned he appeared to have amassed unexpected wealth which enabled him to purchase the ugly featureless cottage on the outskirts of Oxford, which the estate agents had sold for under market value due to the modernisation and repairs needed, which by all accounts were never made. They had expected the property to be prime for demolition and redevelopment of the ample land to furnish a dozen flats for social housing. That of course did eventually happen after the fire, but years after the events so far described.

Another account of his activities came from a lodge to which he had somehow gained admittance. The view from the brethren was that he shunned the more social side of the lodge and progressed to Master Mason fairly quickly. Their view was that he had some ulterior motive for membership and his private personality was drawn to the secretive nature of the fraternity but had ultimately found Freemasonry unsatisfactory and withdrew almost as quickly as he had entered. The brethren reported that he took his masonic duties very seriously and remember his raising from Fellowcraft to Master Mason as being an emotional affair (as it often can be) with Steinberg genuinely engrossed and distressed at the story.

What had been overlooked in the rather poor investigation into the incident in the church was that abomination propped up by the altar. The thing, as anyone with any passing interest in occultist history would recognise, was the Sabbatic Goat as pictured by Eliphas Levi in 1856 and given the ancient name Baphomet. It was that name that would be key to the events that followed. It was as late as 1966 before that same image became synonymous with the name Satan but the link to the occult went back to the Crusades and the persecution of the Templar Knights by King Philip IV of France on Friday 13th October 1307 and their very peculiar confessions.

Philip had many French Templars simultaneously arrested, and then tortured into confessions of over one hundred charges of blasphemy, heresy, spitting and urinating on the cross, and sodomy. Most of the charges were undoubtedly false, but one, that of simulated worship of a heathen idol named Baphomet did indeed form part of a Templar initiation ritual. The description of the object changed from confession to confession. Some Templars denied any knowledge of it. Others, under torture, described it as being either a severed head, a cat, or a head with three faces. The persecutors viewed the Templars adoration of it as worshiping it as their god and saviour, saying that it could save them and that it bestowed on the order all its wealth, made the trees flower, and the plants of the earth to sprout forth. There were stories about a head or two heads, or a carved stone or wooden head on which the figure of Baphomet was painted. Templars were accused of worshipping it by kissing its feet, and exclaiming, 'Yalla'. Was it the head of John the Baptist? Was it the Mandilion, the folded cloth bearing the face of Christ later to be rediscovered as the Shroud of Turin? Was it the image of a daemon, or something else entirely? It was this image, this creature, this idol that became the fascination for Steinberg and he dedicated the rest of his life to the quest for the ultimate truth regarding it. What he found and the repercussions were far from what other experts in the field would have expected or wished for, but precisely what Steinberg was after.

Part II: The expeditions

It must have been around 2004 when Steinberg had made further trips back and forth to a number of specific locations in Israel, the West Bank and Egypt. The following year lead him to a trip to the north west of Scotland before numerous journeys back to his parents' native Canada, specifically, Oak Island. It was during the final trip he brought something back.

There were known secret labyrinths on Oak island, once thought to contain pirate treasure. What had he found buried there? The first clues came from a discussion with Meredith Joaanas, an amateur archaeologist who he had met online. The two had exchanged emails before embarking together on that final expedition.

From 2004, the pair had written many emails, sent as encrypted documents. The documents had been deleted by both parties by 2007 but when Joaanas' laptop was recovered, remnants were able to be retrieved. It made it harder to piece together what their intentions were and what brought Steinberg to the Middle East, then Scotland before making the discovery on Oak Island.

Here are a few retrieved remnants, neither the chronological order nor which of the two were the writer are known for certain:

"You realise we are on the trail of that phantom of all terrors, Ahriman of the Persians Suteckh, the Typhonian Beast of the Egyptians, the Python of the Greeks, the old serpent of the Hebrews, the fantastic monster, the nightmare, the accuser, the Croquemitaine, the gargoyle, the great beast of the Middle Ages. We are close to finding the bearded idol of the alchemist, the obscene deity of Mendes, the goat of the Sabbath real Baphomet of the Templars…"

"'Baphomet'" may derive from the Arabic word أبو فهمت Abu fihamat, meaning 'The Father of Understanding'. You are right that it can be interpreted as the Greek word 'Sophia' as in 'wisdom'. The link to the prophet Mohammed as 'Mahomet' is a misnomer. The Templars wouldn't create an idol that honoured their enemy. They were trained to 'spit on the cross' as part of an initiation in case of capture, they would be able to fein blasphemy in mind without betraying Christ in their hearts. Philip failed to understand this difference."

"The image is always an hermaphrodite, depicted having two heads or two faces, always with a beard, but in other respects female attributes. Symbols and inscriptions often accompany the image such as serpents, the sun and moon, and other strange emblems."

"There is a theory that suggests that Baphomet is a compound of the words 'baphe' from baptism and 'metis', meaning wisdom. It implies again that the Templars were privy to a secret knowledge. This could point to the Templars being gnostics as you suggest."

"I agree that the Gnostics had much in common with the Pythagoreans. Gnosis of course means 'knowing'. From the prayers recited, according to the diagram of the Ophite-worshippers, when on their return to God they are stopped by the Archons. That is what has always interested me."

They discussed Holy relics. It appeared that part of their quest was a grand unifying theory as hinted at in this message. Again, we do not know the order of these accounts:

"If we talk about sacred relics there are the big ones: the Ark of the Covenant, the box that housed Moses' tablets engraved with the Ten Commandments and operated as a sort of gold-plated radio to God. There's the cross of the crucifixion of Christ, but the one that everyone seems to go on about is the Holy Grail. But no-one can agree on what it is. Some say a cup that Jesus drank from and passed around at the last supper. Some say it caught the blood of Christ at the crucifixion. If it was either of those it would be a small wooden bowl, not a jewel-encrusted golden goblet as depicted in the Dark Ages through to the middle ages. Then there's the idea that Dan

Brown stole about the Holy Grail, that it was the bloodline of Christ via Mary Magdalen. These ideas are vague and wishful simplistic thinking. But there is another less talked about idea that makes it intrinsically linked with our artefact."

"The word 'grail' means 'the transformer of consumable material', hence the link to the cup of Jesus' last supper which contained the wine transubstantiated into the blood of Christ."

Experts have highlighted the following passages as the later ones and key to what Steinberg was looking for:

"The Gnostics described it, based upon writings in the Jewish esoteric book of Zohar (meaning splendour and radiance) which is part of the Kabbalah as well as the book of Exodus. The Kabbalah was kept secret until the 13th Century. It was called the Othiq Yomin or Shekhina in the Zohar. It sustained the Israelites during their life in the desert, providing them with the supernatural food stuff, 'manna'. It was kept or connected to the box of the Ark of the Covenant.

Those were the only few sections from what experts suggested were a much longer discourse between the two that could be retrieved from Joaanas' laptop after her death.

According to the Old Testament book 'Exodus', after their escape from bondage in Egypt, Moses led the people Israel through the Sinai desert. The people complained that there was nothing to eat. Moses prayed to God and an edible sustenance was provided. Every morning the mysterious Manna appeared. The flaky, wafer-like material had to be cooked and eating that day or it would rot, producing a diabolical smell and become quickly infested with maggots. No other similar journeys through deserts have ever included the miraculous arrival of free food in the same manner as manna. The relevant Bible verses, from the Old Testament are as follows from Exodus chapter 16:

Verse 13: "And when the dew had gone up, there was on the face of the wilderness a fine, flake-like thing as fine as frost on the ground."
Verse 21: "but when the sun grew hot, it melted."
Verse 31: "It was like coriander seed, white, and the taste of it was like wafers made with honey."
Verse 35: "The people of Israel ate the manna forty years, till they came to a habitual land."

Joaanas and Steinberg had seemingly met only the once, on Oak Island, an expedition from which she would not return. But something did return with Steinberg and was installed in his Oxfordshire cottage. Thus began an era of reported strange noises surrounding the cottage. Deliveries were frequently made to the house, but Steinberg was never seen leaving nor entering. A few glimpses of what he was working on during the years 2007 to 2010 were obtained from charred remnants of his journals, retrieved from the later fire:

"I am close! The accounts from the Zohar I obtained in Egypt surpass all later copies I found in Israel. The price was worth it. Combined with the Gnostic accounts and the three surviving parts from the original Perpetual Machine I am close to building my own!"

It appears that the books of Exodus and the Zohar agree on many points by disagree on others. Exodus has no mention of such a machine, the manna appears each morning 'on the ground'. Some experts believe this lack of evidence disproves the machine theory, some suggest that the Zohar oral tradition contains the details which were deliberately kept out of the written record.

There were sections in his journals that detailed the construction of this 'machine'. Some surviving sections showed the text from the Zohar or other ancient documents among with Steinberg's translation into the construction instructions he was following.

Original: The dew of the white head drops into the skull of the small-faces one and is there stored.
Translation: The moisture drops from the perspex dome to the fungal cultivation vessel.

Original: Many shining eyes which shone in many colours. In his lower eyes there are a left and a right eye, and these two have two colours, except when they are seen in the white light of the upper eye.

Translation: Considerable number of control lamps which light up in various colours.

Original (part): It had in its eye sockets carbuncle-eyes, which shone with the brilliance of Heaven, and it was believed to be Shekhina... Its skin had half a beard in its face and the other half in its behind, which was a repugnant thing.... The bald head glittered like gilded silver...

Translation (part): The complete machine was seen as a deity with male and female parts.... At the top was a dew-distilling apparatus which consisted of a curved, cooled surface over which air flowed, condensing the water.... The water made its way to the centre where it was the supply for the fungal yeast growth which underwent gas exchange of oxygen and carbon dioxide to hydrolyse the starch in the yeast giving a malt-like taste to the manna.... The machine was powered by a small nuclear reactor, stored within the Ark of the Covenant. The Ark powered the machine which ran continuously....

Steinberg's hypothesis had become clear. He had identified Baphomet as a machine, powered by the Ark, which had sustained the people Israel for forty years. The machine was given to Moses, or the instructions for its construction and repair, by God, or perhaps by agents of God, translated by the Gnostics as 'angels' or 'watchers'.

After the exit from the desert, the device was kept in the Ark in the Tabernacle before eventually being placed in the specially built temple in Jerusalem by Hiram Abiff for King Soloman. The temple was destroyed five hundred years later by the Babylonians. On learning of this six hundred years later during the Crusades, a special order of knights were founded at the temple ruins with the aim of retrieving the 'grail' which Steinberg now identified it as the Ark and Manna Machine together, as he called it 'The Perpetual Machine'. This was Baphomet, discovered by the Templars Knights who managed to transport at least the top of it, the 'head', out of the Middle East, first to France and then defying persecution, smuggled it to Scotland where it was shipped to Oak Island in Canada in 1398. Now, after a story of 3200 years, Steinberg and Jaanson had unearthed the remains of the machine, with Steinberg returning what parts they found back to Oxford before beginning a reconstruction process with the aim of building a working version of the device.

We now know of course that he was successful in that aim and that the parts of the original device recovered from Canada ensured that it worked all too well and in an unexpected way, not discussed since the earliest accounts described in Exodus, which is what Steinberg was really after all along.

Part III: Call of the Archons

There is little doubt that sometime during 2009 Steinberg became the first man to taste manna for over three thousand years. Later, following up on the deliveries that were made to the house it was found that all food deliveries stopped around that time and for the last a few months of that year, Steinberg survived on manna alone. From his journal:

"The device has few controls. It seems clear to be now that with the resonance correct I can call above the eighth sphere, to Sophia, to Barbelo, beyond the wall of tri-dimensional space to the supercelestial regions, beyond the seven dimensions of Hebdomad which lie above to see His face!"

There followed a garbled and disgusting account of the early experiments of his youth, detailing where he had made mistakes before. He had tried every disgraceful method through occult means, fusing ritual, sex, sacrificial animals, the use of human remains with obscure techniques of quantum electrodynamics and gravitational magnetism, to capture information from beyond the normal dimensions of space and time. Some of these sickening endeavours had limited success, converting the spin of multi-dimensional photons to create distorted photographic images from the beyond. With the perpetual machine now at his disposal was able to do all of that and more. He really did believe that he could use the device to speak directly to God.

He had chosen the 31st October, All Hallows Eve for his final experiment, perhaps symbolically, perhaps because he believed that the worlds are indeed closer together on that night. He set up a video camera to capture the momentous event. The SD card recorded what happened. Very few have seen the footage. The following transcript was made from it. The card was to be copied and the footage analysed further but it mysteriously went missing. Rumour has it someone stole it to sell, perhaps for broadcast, perhaps to a private collector. No known copies exist.

The camera showed the perpetual machine. In the half light and glow from its own control lights it did resemble a humanoid form. It was flanked by wire trunking and a plethora of other devices, a computer server and a capacitor and transformer array. The darkened room looked more like the inside of an electrical power substation. One or more of the parts retrieved from the original Ark may have been the final transducer that enabled the set up to function as some sort of communication device. The camera was mounted on a tripod with Steinberg's back to it.

"Now I can finally do it. I can do what Moses did on Mount Sinai and call upon Him! The final preparations are nearly ready. El Shaddai! Allah! Adonai! Elohim! Jehovah! Creator! The Great Architect! Sabaoth! I call you!"

We can't ever be sure how the machine worked and what its operating and control mechanisms are from the video footage. It appeared that Steinberg was scaling through some kind of step up tuning mechanism, not dissimilar from a television or radio signal. Steinberg began to get frustrated that there wasn't enough power. There was clearly something amiss. On the recording he can be heard muttering about being stuck in the realms of Hebdomad (ἑβδομάς) which in Gnostisim denotes the name of seven world creating dimensions of the archons, the archons being angelic-type beings, lower than God, called the watchers and fallen angels of the Old Testament. They are believed to be semi-hostile powers, and are the last and lowest emanations of the Godhead. Below them and derived from them comes the low level sphere of the dimension of the demonic powers.

The noises emanating from the machine, accompanied by arcing of electricity reached a climax and the room suddenly became filled with a different kind of light, almost purple. The shock caused Steinberg to stumble backwards, knocking the camera tripod slightly. But it could still be seen: there in the centre of the room stood a blurred and shaking winged apparition. It was around eight feet tall, crouching on its legs, only just fitted into the room. It's three horned head goat-like face glared straight at the camera just before the photoreceptor in the camera was burnt out.

Power cuts were reported across Oxfordshire that night. Those near to the cottage reported hearing queer unearthly noises like the sound of large some tortured animal.

There was one eyewitness of the fire that night. Charles Smith looked up to the windows of the cottage and was terrified to hollow faces with gaping open mouths and sunken dark spaces for eyes, crowding around every window, both upstairs and downstairs. He reported that he did not see the splayed figure of a man, collapsed face down on the lawn. The heat prevented him getting close enough to consider entering the building, but he admitted that the faces felt malevolent and he had the desire to run away from the area. His dog disappeared that night and was never seen again.

Fortunately, after the fire not much remained of the machine due to the intense inferno. No radioactive traces were found so Steinberg must have powered the device through traditional electrical means and created the high tension needed using super capacitors. The few remnants from his journals and the SD card were the only clues retrieved from the debris of the cottage. The site was bulldozed soon afterwards and cleared to make way for a development of seven modern dwellings.

The figure discovered by the fire brigade on the lawn was Steinberg. The postmortem showed deep claw marks to his chest and that the burns sustained to his face and hands were not due to the fire, but rather to an intense and sustained radioactive glare. His foolish quest had stopped way short of reaching God, or even the messengers of God who had first delivered the Grail/Ark/Manna

Machine/Shekhina to Moses millennia ago. Instead through his twisted occult means had unintentionally summoned an archonic daemon.

The Oxford Mail ran a short piece the following week about the death of Oxford's 'Real Harry Pottter', the 43 year old occultist who had died in a house fire. There was a brief re-run of the story from ten years ago and the same photograph. No reference was made to any other part of the story and a week later it was all forgotten.

Part V: Epilogue (from BBC news)

In 2015 a bronze statue was unveiled in Detroit. It is nearly 9ft tall and depicted a winged hermaphrodite known as Baphomet, flanked by two smiling children. It cost £64,000 to make and hundreds of Satanists turned out to see it unveiled. The Satanic Temple plans to move the piece 900 miles south-west and erect it opposite a Ten Commandments monument outside Oklahoma City's Capitol Building. Baphomet will "complement and contrast" the Christian commandments which include "unconstitutional prohibitions against free speech and free exercise of religion," according to the organisation. Two fingers on the right hand point up and two on the left hand point down, meaning 'as above, so below'.

"Our statue will serve as a beacon calling for compassion and empathy among all living creatures," said Lucien Greaves, the group's co-founder.

On the back of the idol was a stone slab engraved with a passage from Lord Byron's *Cain*, that read, "Then who was the Demon? He who would not let ye live, or he who would have made ye live forever, in the joy and power of knowledge?"

References:
Sassoon, G. und Dale, R.: The Manna-Machine, Sidgwick & Jackson, London 1978.
Sassoon, G. und Dale, R.: The Kabbalah Decoded, Duckworth, London 1978.
Fiebag, J. und P.: Die Entdeckung des Heiligen Grals, Goldmann, München 1989.

Ghosts

On the Shores of Lake Onyx and other weird tales

Ghosts

Should you believe in ghosts? What evidence is there for them? How are they supposed to work? Billions of people have died. Why aren't we overrun with them? Ghost experts say that ghosts are only formed when people die unexpectedly (so that must include everyone who died in their sleep) or those that died through violence (Flanders, Ypres and the Somme must be swarming with them) or through unfinished business (so that must be everyone, I mean who has 'finished business'?)

There should be millions and millions of ghosts all over the place. Every single city, town or village should be inundated with them. But all we get is garbled reports of a 'grey lady' or 'headless monk' or sightings of a Roman soldier or a cup of tea moving from where someone thought they put it to somewhere else. There should be around three thousand of them haunting hundreds of feet in the air above ground zero. There should be tens of thousands in Hiroshima, hundreds of thousands, if not millions, around Auschwitz. But no. There are none. Instead we get silence and quietness in those places. The ghosts, if they are there, keep out of sight, they make no noise, they keep their secrets. They don't want to talk to you. They probably don't even see you.

In Britain, the ghosts you do hear about seem to be from particular times too. You don't get many modern ghosts. You're unlikely to hear about a ghost of a rocker from the 1950s, which is a shame. They're usually Victorian, or seventeenth century, maybe an Elizabethan or the odd Roman soldier. There isn't much in the way of pre-Roman ghosts, even though people must have lived on these islands for well over ten thousand years. Plus, the stories that 'cause' them to be ghosts don't seem that, well, that powerfully violent or horrid compared to the everyday violence and horror that occurs in contemporary times: the bride that died on her wedding day, the family feud, the disgraced monk or the failed artist with the failed relationship.

Then there's the evidence for these ghosts, or lack of it. Like the ghost photo. The advent of Photoshop consigned the worst type of photo manipulation and obvious double exposure to the dustbin of history. It's hard to believe any photo these days and yet the ones that remain 'unexplained' are, like UFO photos, grainy, indistinct, often black and white and, well, rubbish. 'At the rear of the Great War group photo of the battalion is the face of the young corporal who died the previous day'. Or the photo was taken the previous week. Or the face at the back was someone who was late for the lineup, or wasn't supposed to be there. 'The man in the back of the car was her late husband who had died the previous year' or was due to die the following year. We're taking the story as fact without any facts or the dating of anything.

There's a favourite of mine of the girl in a strange out-of-time school uniform with a ribboned boater hat, although the picture was taken in the early 1980s. She has no legs. She appears to be floating through the crowd, not quite in focus, with a deathly pale face and haunting expression. The photo was hailed as a genuine ghost photo for years, until the arrival of the internet when the girl (now a woman) in question saw herself in the photo and pointed out that she was very much alive and that day had been rushing through the crowd, late in meeting up with her friends.

There's the Brown Lady of Raynham Hall. The story that forms the ghost is less than spectacular. Supposedly it is of Lady Dorothy Walpole, the sister of Prime Minister Robert Walpole. When her violent second husband Townshend discovered she had slept with Lord Wharton, he punished her by locking her in her rooms. She apparently remained at the house at Raynham Hall until her death, many years later, in 1726, from smallpox. The ghost was first seen in 1835, once in 1836 then not again until 1917 and then again in 1926. It was always in the room in which her painting hung, wearing a brown dress. It was in 1936 when the famous staircase photo was taken of what appears to be a hooded figure of light descending the stairs. Perhaps. Or perhaps a smear on the lens, or an unusual falling of light from the window giving a false sense of perspective. It could even be, as some have suggested a simple double exposure, accidental or deliberate. If this is all we have, it is far from conclusive.

As I wrote that last sentence, the front door slammed shut. I wasn't aware the front door was open. How did that happen? Who is it that has gone? I finish the bottle and take my pills.

Ghost photos can't be real (even if ghosts are, which I doubt). Whatever ghosts are, they cannot be photographed. The evidence is simple. Over the past decade, the number of people carrying cameras has risen exponentially. So too has the number of people willing and able to share interesting images over the internet. A genuine, clear, provable ghost photo would be transmitted around the world in a matter of minutes. But it hasn't happened. With all these photographers, armed with a camera for every situation, no new ghost photos have appeared. Oh, there's plenty of camera straps, digital anomalies and spirit orbs (fine particulates like dust or pollen caught in the flash of a cheap digital camera with the flash too close to the lens). But not one genuine ghost.

All we have is half-baked anecdotal stories that seem to include or borrow from each other. The famous 'ghost tour' type begin with 'it's said that she haunts the corridors at night, searching forever for her baby'. Then there's the urban myth type 'my friend's friend heard a story about her friend's uncle who's sister once saw the headless nun walking past the window'. The most gruesome are those people who were bricked up in the walls of the house, only to find that even in death they were trapped. Then there's the suicides. What a bummer, to try to escape your crummy life only to become a ghost and have to go through it all over and over again, for ever.

It's getting dark again. I don't go out in the day, it's too bright. I wear what I always wear. I don't recall wearing anything else. But if I do I suppose I can just change it. Off I go for my short walk down to the canal. The pills are starting to work. There's no-one around. I can't remember ever seeing anyone. I don't believe in people. What evidence is there for people? The water is dark as it always is. But it's not cold anymore. Perhaps it was once, I can't remember. Perhaps this is all there is, just this ghost of what once was. Is that something I should believe in?

Night School

On the Shores of Lake Onyx and other weird tales

Night School

I didn't tend to work late. There was always plenty to do of course as any teacher will tell you, work doesn't finish at 3:15. There's the marking, the lesson planning, which I think could be greater in science than other subjects because we have to think about what experiments we want to run a week or more in advance and order all the equipment. I have twelve classes of twenty eight kids. That's twenty three new lessons to deliver each week to three hundred and thirty six kids. Each class has one homework a week and the school expects that marked as well as stuff in their books along with quality feedback and targets set for each student. (We called them students now, not pupils. Just as we say 'academy' now not 'school'). So there's plenty to do. I just don't tend to do it in the classroom. Usually I'll head into town and work in my favourite bookshop till they close at six. But that day I stayed on in my lab to set up some wall displays and hang models of planets and spaceships from the ceiling, that year seven had made. It was October so the darkness was drawing in, not that I'd notice in the lab. During a five period day, unless you're on break duty, you don't really see the outside. In the new science block there was no need to leave for any reason; reprographics was downstairs, the department staff room was at the end of the corridor as was the prep room. There wasn't time to visit the main staff room in the old building and I had a packed lunch, that I sometimes found time to eat. So I didn't notice the sun had set. But I did notice, out of the corner of my eye that the far corner of the lab was dark, or darker than my subconscious felt it should be. I looked over. The fluorescent down lighters were all on. The room was evenly lit. I went back to cutting the nylon thread to the appropriate length to hang a Saturn V rocket from the ceiling. It happened again. I felt that the far corner of the room was darker. I wasn't even facing that way. Before I minded to turn around I thought I heard a voice.

'Sir?' it said, or I thought it said.

There was no-one there. My lab had connecting doors to the adjacent labs on either side. I opened them and looked in. No-one was there. The lights were off. There would often be a colleague staying on to do their preparation, but not that night. Was it a student hanging around? Unlikely. Detention was Wednesday, this was Tuesday. Few kids hung around past 3:30, unless they had to.

I looked around the lab again. Everything was as it should be. The lab was clean and tidy, everything in the room was new, with the formica coated grey desks and matching cupboards and grey vinyl floor. Behind my front desk was the whiteboard and projection screen. It was all a far cry from when I was at school. Wooden benches etched with the graffiti from generations earlier and stained with the hydrochloric acid of a thousand experiments. The teacher would be at the front, chalk in hand (no projections then, not even overhead projectors like we had later at university). We'd sit there and hang on every word, and copy every word down eagerly into our books, in neat cursive handwriting with our fountain pens.

'Sir?' the voice said again, clearer this time. I looked up. The room was suddenly dark except for a glow at their end. It was as if the room, or my vision had become a tunnel. All I could see or focus on was a circle of light at the far end in which sat a young boy.

'Can you explain it again sir?' he said. He must have been 13 or 14. His uniform was wrong, no purple jumper and single coloured house tie. He had a blue and silver striped tie (and I could see it was a proper one, not a clip on) and a dark blue blazer.

'The motor effect sir?' he said. There was something familiar about the voice, a soft northern accent, not the Oxford accent of around here. He seemed blurred, I couldn't make out the face, pale, young, open. It felt dreamlike. I wanted to be startled, I wanted to ask who he was, to walk towards him. I couldn't.

'Yes of course,' I said instead and turned towards the board but paused to pick up a board pen. There wasn't one anywhere at first and then I saw one on a tray at the base of the board that I hadn't ever had before. I picked it up. It had no cap so probably wouldn't work. As I raised my head to place the pen on the white board I found that I held in my hand a piece of white chalk against a dusty blackboard. I spun around to the student and felt a rush of vertigo as if I could fall down the tunnel towards him. Then the room returned to normal. The lighting was even, the boy gone, the whiteboard as it should be and a dried up whiteboard marker in my hand.

I didn't mention the episode to anyone. Two uneventful weeks passed and then it happened all over again. The tunnel of light, the pupil, his voice, and in my hand was a piece of chalk. This time I drew on the board. It was a diagram of a D.C. motor: the magnets and the field labelled N and S, the circular wrapped wire with the current direction labelled. At right angels to these was the direction of movement of the wire due to the force generated by the current flowing through the flux of the magnetic field... The boy stayed that same distance away and I couldn't, for some reason, walk towards him. All I could see was that he was making notes. Good notes. He asked questions and I answered. I don't know how long the 'session' lasted. But, just as before, it abruptly ended and then everything was as it was before.

Again I told no-one. From that point it happened every week at the same time. I taught him nuclear fission, parallax of the stars, acceleration under gravity, all sorts. I taught and he listened. I tried to rationalise it. Was I hallucinating? We all get tired in this job. Why me? Or has it happened to other teachers, only they never said (just as I hadn't)? Was it a ghost? The building was new, and there hadn't been a building on the site with the same dimensions and orientation. Why was I being sought out by this... whatever it was?

It went on for three months. I can't say that I wanted it to stop. There was something rewarding about it. I got more enthusiastic as it went on, better at explaining, better at answering his questions, better at knowing what he needed.

It was close to Christmas. We were discussing light. I think it was the topic that reminded me of how unusual this all was. For the first time since that initial encounter I was more conscious of the tunnels and the surreal nature of it all. I tried to focus on him. He was sat at a wooden bench, not the modern new desks we have here. I tried to focus on his face, but had that blurred, moving, out of the corner of your eye feeling. I took a few steps closer, but as I stepped away from the blackboard it was not just a feeling of vertigo but an actual sense of falling, falling towards him. I lost my footing and seemed to accelerate right at him. I put out my hands to avoid a collision, my face seemed to be directed straight at his. In that final moment when we should have smacked into each other I saw his face clearly. It was familiar. It was me.

I picked myself up off the floor, the floor of the normal, perfectly ordinary twenty-first century lab. I still have no explanation and I've never told anyone. I think of it now as a personal CPD session I attended, re-training myself somehow. The images, manifestations and the version of myself from 1985 never re-appeared again.

On the Shores of Lake Onyx and other weird tales

The Ghost of Tracey Pemberton

On the Shores of Lake Onyx and other weird tales

The Ghost of Tracey Pemberton

I had never seen death. But the idea of the danger of death and of violence seemed to be all around us back then. There were rumours that some kids down a particular street had poured petrol over a boy's head and set fire to him. There were rumours that so-and-so's brother was a granny killer. He'd killed her with the broom he had been using to sweep the streets with by shoving it up her arse. But there was nothing that disturbed me more than the mysterious disappearance of Tracey Pemberton that autumn, all those years ago.

The first we heard about it was when the police came to school to tell us she had gone missing. It was only then that we'd noticed she'd gone, although it had been three days by then. It was the same two policemen who had come to tell us not to play with fireworks a couple of years ago. An older kid in the village had emptied the powder from a box of fireworks into a metal toolbox and threw in a match. It ripped half his face off. Last year, the same policemen came to tell us not to play on the railway line. They told us about the boy who'd got run over by a train and was spread three miles down the track like paté. Sensible kids, if they existed, would have thought that was a big enough deterrent to avoid the railway line. Gerald Baker said that if you put your ear to the track you could hear if a train was coming, which is what the Red Indians did, he said, so some kids went off to try that. But when they'd got there a man had decided to kill himself by hanging himself from the railway bridge that went over the waste ground. Of course it was John Bradford who found the body, hanging there, spinning as the trains went past. He and a couple of other kids were arrested. Apparently a load of them had got bored listening to the rails and had attempted to lay a sleeper across the tracks to derail a train.

In this assembly we were told about the last movements of Tracey Pemberton. Had we seen her? We hadn't. All the teachers wore worried faces. Lillian Goldberg was exempt from assembly because she was Jewish so she wasn't allowed to sing All Things Bright and Beautiful with us but she was allowed to come in after as they wheeled in the big TV when it was time to watch the stranger video.

The main premise was that everyone you knew was good and everyone you didn't know probably wanted to torture and kill you. But they were clever, these strangers. They hung around the school gates tempting kids into their Ford Granadas with the offer of sweets, or an irresistible invitation to come and look at some puppies or kittens (we all groaned, whoever fell for that trick deserved to be tortured).

The latest tactic though was that they would say your mother was ill and that they would offer to pick you up, posing as a neighbour or long lost uncle. To survive this threat we were told to have a password, known only to our ourselves, our mothers and our real uncles. The video said we could use the name of our teddy bears. Mine was called 'Teddy' so I figured that wouldn't be too useful. I started thinking of some obscure character from Star Wars that no-one would guess and then longed for the opportunity to test a suitable stranger who would never be able to ascertain that it was the bounty hunter Dengar, and be caught out.

The other place strangers would lurk was on the merry-go-round in play areas. Had Tracey been at the play area? No, she hadn't we said. The video warned that strangers actually looked quite normal, just like ordinary people and not at all like the monsters they really were. To demonstrate this the film showed a stranger sat on a roundabout in a playground. The roundabout rotated slowly round to reveal a hideously deformed monstrous face.

'If strangers looked like this,' said the video, 'you'd know not to talk to them.'

Lillian Goldberg and a few others cried at this point and were led out. Even I had a lump in my throat, haunted by that sudden reveal of the stranger monster in the playground, and forevermore expecting everyone I didn't know to pull off their fake human visage to reveal a writhing maggot infested melted monster face like Doctor Who monsters Magnus Greel or Scaroth of Jaggaroth (both who, incidentally, kidnapped and tortured people).

So we had to be on our guard and report anything suspicious to the police. Or if we remembered anything at all, to talk to a policeman. This call to arms was all we needed to begin our own investigation. If Tracey was out there, we'd find her. If she had been caught and killed by some stranger, we'd hunt him down and make him pay.

That night me, Spud, Harry and Kirky were out playing with Spud's Action Man tank, rolling it down the hill. Then it got too dark and Harry went home, so we walked around to the edge of the village and there was Nicolas. He was a good few years older than us, he might have been fourteen or fifteen. He wasn't allowed to go to our school anymore because he'd hit a girl. It didn't make sense to me because people were hitting and being hit all the time, and if it was the girl I thought it was, it didn't surprise me. I don't think he had been to another school since as we'd seen him hanging around outside the school railings during the day over the past few years and we'd always shout 'hello' to him.

'All right lads,' said Nicolas. 'That's a good tank. Has it got a motor?'

'No, it hasn't,' said Spud.

'I used to have one with a motor. Went really, really fast. Brilliant it was. Got any tabs?' said Nicolas.

'Nar, we don't smoke' said Kirky.

'Very wise, very wise,' said Nicolas. 'We're you going?'

'Oh, we don't know,' I said. 'We're looking for clues, you know.'

'Yeah, we're investigating.' said Kirky.

'What, you looking for the missing girl?' said Nicolas.

'Yeah. Do you know anything?' said Spud.

'She was pretty,' said Nicolas. 'A pretty girl. Pretty girls shouldn't be out at night. It's dangerous. If I was a girl I'd wear trousers, you know, to look like a boy so you wouldn't get caught.'

'Caught by who?' I said.

'I dunno. No-one. Maybe the tramp up the hill,' said Nicolas. 'That's who I think dunnit. But my dad say it was the gypos. Anyway, I'm going now.'

With that he started walking back to the crossroads.

'What do you think?' said Spud. 'Is there a tramp on the hill?'

'I heard there was,' said Kirky. 'Wasn't there an escaped mental patient or something? Didn't he live up there in a cave?'

'There are a few caves up there,' said Spud. 'Let's go at the weekend.'

My younger brother and I walked to school on Friday, the next day, meeting Spud halfway and one of my brother's friends. We had to cross the patch of rough ground, covered in brambles and rubble where some old wooden buildings had once stood. On the clearest, flattest part there was the battered brown caravan of the gypsy family. In front of it was the blackened remains of a fire with a structure over it that held a large cauldron. The door to the caravan was open and the gypsy man stood there on the steps being spoken to by two policemen. Inside a baby was crying. We hurried past.

'I'm not allowed to talk to Nicolas anymore,' said Spud.

'Who's that, the retard?' said my brother's friend.

'Why not?' I said.

'Dunno, my parents told me not to,' Spud said.

There were three gypsy children who came to the school. The twin boys were in the year above us and the girl in the year below. I'd never spoken to them. I don't think they spoke English. At playtime I saw some girls running off laughing leaving the gypsy girl on her own crying. She had long, thick black hair and dark skin. She wore an old-fashioned looking dress with a blue floral pattern. It was a bit torn. The teachers came and took her inside. I think she went home.

It was a steep walk up the hill on Saturday morning to look for the killer's cave. We took the short cut across the chalk face and through the natural paths that ran through the gorse to a bit that levelled off with a small plain of grass, nibbled smooth by wild rabbits. Further up was a batch of thin woodland. Then past that we were at the top which flattened out, a strange unnatural looking area covered in a yellowish sandy earth. I'd heard that it had been used as a Victorian rubbish tip, now all filled in and covered up. We knew that it backed onto a grey slag heap at the other side. It looked like a creepy alien world. What emphasised the strangeness was the odd crater like holes that had appeared here and there. From them issued a warm dusty steam like a dormant volcano. We carefully crossed this wasteland to the ridge, not wanting to fall into a crater and never be seen again. Beyond was an overgrown area which was where the caves might be.

Forcing through the brambles, we found the tramp's cave. Someone had definitely been there and had lit a fire, but a while ago. There were some dirty clothes and rags in the corner. There was no evidence of any murders, no blood or bones, not even any evidence of shackles and forced slavery. There were bits of rusty metal scattered about. I said it looked far more like evidence of a Dalek Invasion of Earth, so we went off and imagined that instead until teatime.

On the way home we saw the man who'd moved into the flat behind Spud's house. I think he worked at the university.

'Hello lads,' he said.

'I think I saw a kitten at your window last night,' said Spud.

'Yes. I just picked her up,' said the man. 'Do you want to come round and see her?'

'Yes, but we can't,' I said, 'Doctor Who's on in a minute.'

'Can we come round tomorrow?' asked Spud.

'What's she called,' I said, trying to hold on to the tiny black and white fluffy kitten.

'Tosca,' said Marc. 'Do you want some juice?'

'Funny name,' said Spud. 'Yes please.'

'Biscuits?' said Marc.

'Yes please,' we said in unison.

'I named her after my favourite Opera,' said Marc, putting down two glasses of blackcurrant and a plate of chocolate biscuits and picking up a record. On the sleeve were big fancy letters in white, 'Tosca'.

'If I named my cat after my favourite record it would be 'The Night Before' from 'Help!'' I said.

'I don't know that one,' said Marc.

'Have you got a wife?' asked Spud.

'No,' said Marc, 'it's just me. That's why I got the kitten. I get a bit lonely.'

We played with the kitten for a while. She was so funny. Then we thought we'd better go.

'Can we see her again?' I said.

'Of course,' said Marc. ' You can come whenever you like.'

'I think Tracey was killed by the witch,' said Shelly on Monday.

'What witch?' I asked.

'You know, the one in that old house that used to be boarded up.'

I knew the one. A thin house, with black window frames that formed one side of the alley that was a short cut through to the estate. On the way home from school, Spud and I crept up to it and looked in the window. First of all I could only see the black grate of the fireplace. To the right it was a rack filled with smallish dumbbells used for weightlifting. Spud knocked on the door.

'Come on, let's go!' he said and made off.

'What?' I said.

The door opened. A massive bare chested bald man stood there scowling. I ran after Spud as the man shouted after us.

There was still no news of Tracey. Her parents had been on TV now, asking for anyone to come forward if they knew anything. We still didn't know anything.

'He's probably got her tied up in a lock up garage,' said Trevor, an older boy, as we left the VG shop with the three penny chews we'd bought using money we'd found in the gutter.

'It's probably him,' said Trevor, pointing to an old man walking down the other side of the road with his dog. 'That's the tramp who killed all those kids years ago. He lives in the cave on the hill.'

The man had unkempt grey hair and beard and wore an old dirty brown coat, fastened closed with a bit of old rope. Another bit of rope was the lead for his Alsatian.

The police had been called to a garage the next day. It was one of the ones up by Wheato's house, a bank of ten, five on each side with flat roofs we'd climbed on and jumped off pretending to be Superman. Each had a different coloured metal door. Now the police had gone, we went to have a look. There was nothing to indicate what had happened.

'It's this one,' said Wheato.

Spud and I starred at the innocuous blue garage door.

'This is the garage he kept his car running in. The hosepipe is still in there. You can see it through this gap,' said Wheato.

I'd only ever heard the word 'suicide' in the lyrics to the song from the television programme M*A*S*H.

'Suicide is painless, it brings on many changes,' went the song. Terry Wogan played it on the radio in his breakfast show on Radio 2 that was always on in our house. I wondered why anyone would want to totally give up on everything. Why would they do it?

'To run away from their problems,' my Dad said.

But to me, it seemed like being dead was a much bigger problem than anything you'd have to face in life.

'He'd taken his own life,' they told us. But he hadn't 'taken' anything anywhere. He'd given up his life, he'd thrown the towel in, thrown his life away, withdrawn from the game. Why do it such a boring way, car fumes in a deserted lock up garage on this estate? I fantasised about how I'd do my own suicide. Jumping off the Cathedral was my best idea, after hanging there precariously for a while to draw a good crowd. Leaving enough time for Mike Neville and the cameras of Look North to arrive before letting go. Barry said it had already been done. We were told the man in the garage had got divorced and lost his job. There was no sign of Tracey.

'Did Tracey's dad kill himself?' I asked Barry.

'No, he died of cancer when she was five,' he said.

To aid in our investigations, Spud and I went to buy ourselves cheap plastic magnifying glasses from the newsagent. Someone pushed past us as we went in.

'Wasn't that Nicolas?' I said, looking out of the shop door. Spud looked too.

'What's happened to him?' said Spud.

His left eye was all black and half closed with other cuts on his head, some with stitches.

'Go away!' he said as we called after him. Once we had our magnifying glasses we went round to see Marc and Toska.

The weather was good throughout that whole autumn and we were out most of the time. At weekends, all the time.

'Come and see the body!' said Harry excitedly as we were thinking what to do next on Saturday morning.

'Body? What body? Where?' I said.

Harry led us off down to the main road out of the village. I don't know what we expected to find, but what Harry pointed to, next to a tree by the side of the road was a large dead dog that had been run over.

'Mad isn't it!' said Harry excitedly.

Someone had thrown a brick onto it. Its guts were spewed out with the brick half inside its belly.

'It's the tramp's dog,' Spud said first, although I knew it too. The rope lead was still around its neck.

On the way home, across the wasteland I saw that the gypsy caravan wasn't there anymore.

The next day, the police were in the school again with Tracey's parents this time. Tracey's mother was holding their new baby which cried all the time. The police had set up an incident room in the community centre so we were used to seeing them about. Tracey's mum had been a pupil at the school. Apparently he had been taught by our teacher, Mr Kean, although he didn't look old enough. He'd once joked that if Tracey hurried up and had a child, he could teach her too and that would mean he'd done three generations. Most of the girls had giggled. I had tried to work this out to see if it was possible and figure out how old he must be and how old Tracey's mum could be but my maths wasn't good enough.

I think some of the girls had a crush on Mr Kean. I can't think why with his BO and coffee breath. He certainly favoured them over us boys. He wore his watch the wrong way round and drove a battered Cortina mark 3.

Some of the older boys had been taken into the headmaster's office for questioning. I knew which ones as she would sometimes hang around with them and older boys from the big school outside the Cross Keys and she'd wear their leather jackets. Tracey's stepdad had so many tattoos on his arms that his skin looked entirely green as if he was a lizard.

'What's a 'queer'?' Spud asked me on the way home.

'I dunno. Is it a poof? A bloke that doesn't want to get married?' I said. 'Why?'

'My Dad says Marc is a queer,' said Spud. 'I'm not allowed to go round there anymore.'

I didn't want to go round to see Toska on my own so I got Kirky to come with me. There was no answer from the doorbell. We heard voices from inside and a thin man with a beard came to the door. He had yellow washing-up gloves on.

'Why don't you bugger off you disgusting animals!' he shouted at us.

We backed away. There was a bucket near the door. My nostrils caught a whiff of bleach.

'Go, on, bugger off!' the man said again. So we did.

The next day I went round to Barry's house to see if he was playing as it had been his birthday. He lived in the council houses at the far side of the village.

'I got an Action Man from my granddad,' he said as we walked off from his house and over to the fields. 'My grandad was in the Army you know and I think he wanted me to be interested too so he thought an Action Man would make me like the idea more.

'So I opened the box, and you know you can't tell what you're going to get until you open it?' he continued.

'Yeah, my first one had brown hair and my second one has

blonde hair. They both have a scar,' I said.

'They all have a scar,' said Barry. 'Anyway, listen. So I open the box and he's so proud and I pull it out and it's a black Action Man. Seriously! So I say, 'wow, thanks grandad, I'm going to have fun playing with this, and he says, 'Er, no, that's not right, I think there's something wrong with it, I'll get you a new one.''

'What really?' I said.

'Yeah, he's a racist. I think he thinks I'm a poof.'

As we walked along we caught sight of hundreds of bits of paper trapped in the hedge that had been blown there by the wind. As we walked on there was a lot more of it, all ripped up. Barry bent down and picked up a few pages. They looked as though they'd been ripped out of glossy magazines. They were all colour photos of naked people, mostly women, some of them doing things to men.

'What shall we do with them?' said Barry after collecting quite a bundle.

'I don't know,' I said.

He shoved them back in the hedge.

She'd been missing two weeks by this point. We were told the chances of her being found alive now were quite slim. Some of us were asked if we wanted some counselling. I said no because I didn't know what that was. The council did the bins so perhaps it was something to do with that.

Tracey wasn't one of the thick ones, you know, she was clever.

She was always getting praised for good work by the teachers, especially Mr Kean. It was sad to think she was dead. I'd played a few playground games with her over the years. She always teased me about my two front teeth. She had long wavy hair, a really friendly smile and a few freckles on her cheeks. I'd held her hand once, long, long ago. This year, she, and most of the girls seemed older and more distant. When we played The Empire Strikes Back in the bike sheds, none of them wanted to join in, not even to play Princess Leia, so Barry had to do that part. I had to do Vader and Luke which meant I was talking to myself for a lot of it.

That night I had a dream about her. I was walking through the shopping arcade and thought I saw her. I lost her in the crowd and then saw her again further off. The crowd thinned out so that when I'd got round the corner, there she was walking away by herself. I ran over to her shouting her name and put my hand on her shoulder. She turned around. Her face was pale and her eyes blank and hollow. She looked dead. I woke up in a cold sweat.

We had a vigil in the village church. There were lots of candles, prayers and sad hymns. Tracey's older stepbrother arrived on his motorbike and patrolled the area, staring at everyone as if that would force a confession out of them. He kept looking around to see who wasn't singing hard enough as if that was an expression of guilt. The baby cried all the way through.

We walked through the graveyard back home after the service.

It was quite dark. Out of the corner of my eye I kept thinking I was being watched. I thought I saw a pale figure in a white dress beckoning to me from behind a gravestone.

On the news there was an announcement that they'd found a body. It was found in a shallow grave in some woods near Carlisle. My parents were looking very solemn. I started to laugh. Then went to the toilet and was sick.

The next day, everything at school carried on as normal. How could everyone just carry on as normal? At break time the news spread that the body wasn't hers. It was an old man. How they couldn't have figured that out before I didn't understand. This news brought the relief that it wasn't her and fear as she was still out there somewhere, lost. I couldn't stop thinking about her face. Her face and death. I thought I was going to die, that death is inevitable and I don't have much time left. I became fearful of going to school. In Maths, Mr Kean had us all standing up. He asked us various mental maths questions. If you got it right you sat down. Lillian sat down.

'What's seven times six,' said Mr Kean and indicated it was my question. I hesitated. I couldn't concentrate. I mumbled a wrong answer so had to stay standing. Spud sat down with his question. I got my next one wrong too and had to stand on my chair. Kirky sat down. He was enjoying picking on me know.

'Can you see this everyone?' said Mr Kean, making an example of me. 'If he'd learnt his number bonds he's be sitting down comfortably by now.'

I got the next one wrong and had to stand on my desk. Barry sat down. Even John Bradford got one right and could sit down. Everyone was then seated but the questions kept coming at me while the others laughed. I thought I'm was going to die, or that I wanted to die, I didn't know which. Mr Kean toyed with making me sit on the wardrobe but settled for having me sit at the front of the class, facing the blackboard for what seemed like the rest of the day, with a pointed hat with a large 'D' on it. I wanted to run away. Or die. Or both. I sat there and thought about how to do it, but even that wasn't satisfying. I didn't feel like jumping off the Cathedral. I dreamt about her that night. She was calling to me again.

I went round to Marc's house one more time. He answered the door and said sorry for his friend shouting at us. He said he knew it wasn't me who put the dog dirt through the letterbox. He didn't invite me in though, but he told me that Tosca was dead.

'She fell off one of the kitchen cupboards and landed awkwardly, breaking a leg. She was crying out in such pain that I had to put her to sleep,' he said.

This seemed unlikely. Cats always land on their four paws.

'Did you take her to vet?' I asked.

'It was in the early hours of the morning so I couldn't,' Marc said.

I didn't want to ask how he had done it. Did he use a knife and slit her throat? Did he drown her in the sink? How could anyone do that? It seemed so cruel and unfair. The kitten was crying out because it had a broken leg, it didn't need to be killed.

October came and was darker than usual. The police activity had been scaled back. They said they'd exhausted every line of enquiry. I was thinking about Tosca. Maybe whoever it was hadn't meant to kill Tracey but something had gone wrong and they'd gone too far. Maybe it was an accident.

By November no-one talked about Tracey anymore. It had all been forgotten. Then just before Christmas there was a flurry of news. First, Tracey's mum and stepdad were arrested. Then there was something about Tracey's uncle being arrested in France. It turned out that the story was one that no-one had thought of. No-one came to get her, no-one snatched her away. There were no strangers, tramps, queers, retards or gypsies involved. Something had happened at Tracey's home and she'd run away and been met by this uncle who'd taken her to live with him in France. She hadn't been tortured and killed. It was a long lost uncle, her real uncle, her real dad's brother who had done it and she had wanted to go.

All I heard after that was that Tracey went to live with a foster family somewhere near Chester-le-Street. I wondered if I'd ever see her again. Barry said they gave her a new identity so that no-one could find her. Sometimes I think I see her in crowded streets. Sometimes I see her in my dreams, always at a distance. She's smiling now.

On the Shores of Lake Onyx and other weird tales

The Voice in the Dark

On the Shores of Lake Onyx and other weird tales

The Voice in the Dark

'Light is all around us. Even in what we think is the darkest dark we're rescued by a faint glimpse of light, in the distance, a faint glow, the saviour of the lighthouse, the reassurance of the candle and the glory of a new dawn. So you'd think we'd know what light is. I thought I knew, but I knew nothing until I'd seen the Dark and what it's capable of.'

Apparently he'd been rambling like this for hours, since he awoke, in fact. The doctors had felt it better that he talk, as long as he didn't get agitated. For the moment he was calm and that was good. They felt it was just a stream of consciousness, of random nonsense that he spoke. At least the raving of the previous night had ceased. Johnson addressed no-one in particular. Someone was due to come to listen, to hear an explanation. But for now he just talked.

Mel Turner half wished she had set off a lot earlier. The sun had set as she passed York and now she was driving her Mini Cooper over Fylingdales Moor and it was very, very dark. Then the clouds parted as she past the stark pyramid of the RAF Early Warning centre and for possibly the first time ever she realised she was able to star-gaze and drive at the same time, with no glow of a city to wipe out the sparkle from the myriad of stars in the Milky Way above. Soon there were the lights of the harbour town of Whitby below and the dark blackness of the North Sea beyond. She'd come up from Oxford, a near six hour journey, to visit an old friend and ex-colleague in her cottage somewhere near Robin Hood's Bay, to discuss something disturbing and curious. Right up Mel's street. She finally navigated the hills and winding roads down a hill to find a tall woman in flowing clothes, silhouetted under the outside light of a cottage nestled on the edge of a wood. This was Olivia, fellow scientist and one-time friend from their university days. A dog ran out to meet the car.

'You made it!' said Olivia. 'Don't mind Barney," she indicated the scruffy mongrel dog. 'How are you? Come in!'

They moved inside the cottage and tea was made on the Aga.

'How long has it been?' asked Olivia.

'Twenty, twenty-two years?' Mel replied.

'You still have that pink bit!' said Olivia, indicating the pink stripe amongst Mel's mid length auburn hair. Aside from that, she looked pretty sensible in her jeans and short jacket. Olivia on the other hand was dressed like the anti-establishment history that had shaped her: a loose flowing dress, bracelets and necklaces with shoulder length hair she continually flipped over her shoulder.

'And you're a doctor!' Olivia said. 'Have a biscuit.'

'Thanks. A sort of, professor, I know it sounds mad.'

'I wasn't cut out for all that. But I came back to science as you know. Mainly in chemical industries but then got this job up here at the lab. But your stuff, that weird ghost stuff at the nunnery, really interesting. You'll have to fill me in later. That's why I had to get in touch when this happened. I thought you'd be interested.'

'All I know,' said Mel, 'is what everyone knows about Darkside and the search for dark matter.'

'Darkside's not us. That's the Italian one.'

'It's similar though isn't it? You're hoping to directly detect dark matter in the form of weakly interacting massive particles?'

'Yeah. They'd built the original liquid argon time projection chambers near the Gran Sasso mountain in Italy. Their Darkside-50 experiment has been going since 2013. Ours is called Zeplin IV. It operates with three hundred litres of liquid nitrogen keeping cool an eighty-seven kilogram of xenon target mass. That's sort of, we think, where it happened. Whatever it was, I don't know exactly what occured. We'll go and see him in the morning. He's at the John Cook Hospital in Middlesborough.'

Mel looked out of the kitchen window. In daytime she would have marvelled at the beautiful view over the valley down to the sea, but tonight all she saw was herself reflected back in a black mirror. Outside the wind had picked up.

It's extraordinarily difficult to blackout a room. The light always finds a way in. The nurse had even put strips of black insulation tape over the instruments of the machines in the room. There were curtains over the blinds, black cloths taped up, under which had been taped layer upon layer of kitchen foil to the windows. This was a dark room. It even had an airlock of sorts; a darklock where visitors entered from the light of the ward, into the dark anteroom, closing the door to light so that not a single stray photon could sneak into the patient's room with them. Johnson was still talking.

'I'd noticed that my face started to burn in front of my computer screen. It felt warm at first for the first few days, then more like sunburn. It was the same with fluorescent lights, then sunlight too. All light. Why light? What is light but the energy given off by an electron? That's all it is. The energy given off by an electron as it falls back to its normal state after being excited for some reason. That difference in energy as the electron falls from the top of a ladder to the bottom is given off as a packet of energy called a photon. That's what it is. But that's not all that it is.'

The doctors had given him something for the pain but they knew that physical pain was the least of his problems. Something else had happened. Something not normal. Something to do with the experiment. He continued talking as the nurse fumbled around in the dark, attempting to take his blood pressure and temperature with an infra red thermometer.

'Not now. Don't try to touch me,' said Johnson.

'We'll have to do it sometime soon Mr Johnson,' said the nurse. Johnson rambled on.

'Light's a particle, yes, but it's also a wave. We know it's electromagnetic radiation of varying wavelengths from radio waves through microwaves, infra-red heat, the visible rainbow then ultraviolet, x-rays and deadly gamma rays. None of that helps though. It's like knowing that fruit comes in various forms, an apple, a banana, and orange or even an exotic physalis. Knowing those names tells you nothing about where the fruit came from. What made them and why? I know, you'll tell me that light comes from a light bulb, an LED, the Sun, fire or whatever. But that's just like saying that the fruit comes from a tree. It's not an explanation of any depth. If we have no fruit, we have no fruit that's all. If we have no light we do not simply have an absence of light as I once thought. We have, now I've seen it, something so much less, something so much more malevolent and all pervading. But how can I explain the power of the Dark?'

Mel wished they had taken her own car over the moor to the hospital that morning. It was only a fifty minute journey but it felt a lot longer in Olivia's old motor.

'What is this car?' Mel asked over the noise of the engine.

'This is Rosemary. She's a 1970 Triumph Herald. She's been a good friend to me Rosemary has.'

Mel looked over her shoulder. Barney looked wistfully up from the back seat then put his head down again. After some frustration with parking that happens at every hospital, they made their way to the reception, leaving Barney in the car. As they entered someone jumped up from a chair across the room and called out to them.

'Oh hell,' muttered Olivia, 'I'd forgotten about him.'

'Who?' asked Mel.

'Hi! I'm Adam. Adam Jones. I'm a freelance journalist. I write for the Telegraph, Mail and the BBC website.'

'For God sake,' whispered Mel under her breath.

'Sorry?' said Jones.

'Nothing,' said Mel.

'Look, I didn't say you could be here,' said Olivia.

'You know him?' asked Mel.

'Not really. But...' said Olivia.

'It's ok. The lab have said it's ok and I've spoken to the doctors. They just said to wait for you,' said Jones enthusiastically. 'Look, I'll buy you both a coffee.'

'So the guy's allergic to light? Is he some sort of vampire?' said Jones when they'd sat down with their beverages.

'Look, I don't want you here, but since you are here you'd better not make up a load of tosh,' said Olivia.

'What do you think professor Turner?' asked Jones to Mel. 'It's certainly a spooky one.'

Mel rolled her eyes.

'Oh come on, give me something to go on. What was the experiment? What's this 'dark matter' all about and how is it different to so called 'dark energy'? You can't blame me for printing pseudoscience if you, the scientists keep it all so secret. No wonder people believe in conspiracies.'

Jones looked back and forth at the two women. He hadn't been in this position before, with two attractive women, neither of whom had any respect for him, both of whom were far cleverer than him. It made him uncomfortable. Olivia wasn't going to give him anything and sipped her coffee noisily through its froth.

'Ok, look. There is a wide range of astronomical evidence that the visible stars and gas in all the galaxies, everywhere in the universe, including our own galaxy, are immersed in a much larger cloud of non-luminous matter. This 'dark matter', so called because we can't see it, makes up much more of the mass of the galaxy than the material we can see,' Mel was trying to be as helpful as she could in as few words as possible.

'The majority of matter in the universe is non-baryonic. The nature of this non-baryonic component is still totally unknown, and the resolution of all this is of fundamental importance to cosmology, astrophysics, and elementary particle physics. Get it?' said Olivia, speaking quickly and not looking up from her coffee. 'Do you know what a wimp is?'

'I know you're patronising me. But you're not doing yourselves any favours,' said Jones.

'By wimp she means W-I-M-P, it's part of supersymmetry theory, that dark matter is comprised of as-yet-undiscovered Weakly Interacting Massive Particles or WIMP for short, formed in the early Universe and clustered by gravity around ordinary matter,' said Mel. 'They've built a deep underground lab to try to detect them, if they exist, as they'd be the only particles that won't be stopped by the rock above.'

'Ok, I see. So what's 'dark energy'?' said Jones.

'Here's what we know,' said Mel. 'We have our four fundamental forces in nature, the strong and weak forces inside the atomic nucleus that hold the nucleus together and give rise to atomic radiation, the Electromagnetic force which binds electrons to the nucleus to give us molecules, chemistry, electricity and life. All three of these are very strong forces.'

Olivia put down her coffee cup.

'And then there's gravity,' said Olivia, 'It's so weak that a small magnet can overcome the entire gravitation pull of the Earth and lift up a piece of iron.'

'One of our questions is, 'why is gravity so weak?' and why is it only attractive?' continued Mel.

'What do you mean?' asked Jones.

'We believe the Universe is expanding at an accelerated rate, it's speeding up after the Big Bang, not slowing down,' said Olivia. 'Something is speeding it up. Some intrinsic fundamental energy of negative pressure that is the opposite of gravity. We think it might be something new that we can't detect. Something that permeates all of space, sixty-eight percent of the total energy of the Universe in fact.'

'It's one of the most exciting areas of scientific research in the world,' said Olivia.

'But what's it for?' said Jones. 'I mean, what possible use is all this?'

'When we discovered quantum mechanics just over a hundred years ago it was thought to be totally useless. Then suddenly you've got every computer in the world based on it,' said Mel.

'But so far you've got nothing. You don't know anything,' said Jones. 'It just sounds like when there's a flaw in your theories, when there's something you don't understand, you explain it by simply calling it 'dark'.'

'That's about it,' said Olivia.

'There seems to be a dark theme here with our guy who now can't be out of the dark. Shall we go and see him?' said Jones.

The three were met by a nurse and taken through to meet Johnson in the pitch black of his room.

'Why are we frightened of the dark? Are we frightened by the absence of light? Why do we yearn for the light, for dawn, for summer sun? I was diagnosed with photosensitivity, an allergy to light.' Johnson was just as keen to talk to the newcomers as he was to the medical staff. 'But I carried on with my work. I couldn't believe that it was light that was burning me. Even through layers of clothing. I'd only go out at night, being careful. Two minutes of exposure to bright light causes itching then burning as if my skin is on fire. I'd take a lux meter. They said it was a rare blood disorder, erythropoietic protoporphyria or something, thinking my body was producing high levels of porphyrin which supposedly regulates how your body absorbs vitamin D. It's not that. We know it isn't, don't we? It started when I'd been down a few times.'

Mel felt uncomfortable. It was hard having a conversation in the dark. The walls, unseen, seemed to collapse inwards. The room felt oppressive.

'I'd got the job as one of the technicians at the Deep Underground Science Facility in Boulby,' said Johnson. 'I've got various responsibilities, as well as the important bit of measuring the ratio of the light pulse to the size of the charge, there's the general maintenance, topping up the liquid nitrogen, calibrating the mechanisms and checking for signs of rust or wear and tear. I'd been down everyday for about a week, each day getting a little bit more affected by light when I came back up.'

'So what happened down there?' said Mel. 'Talk us through it.'

'Apart from the increasing light allergy, nothing out of the ordinary went on. Then I heard the voices,' said Johnson.

'What voices?' asked Mel.

'At first they were just voices. The power went out, the lights went off. We were more worried about the experiment than us being in the dark. But it felt so much better in the dark. The itchiness had gone. Then the backup came on after a few minutes. But it was when the lights were off that I heard them.'

'So what did these 'voices' say then?' asked Olivia incredulously.

'At first they just wanted to make contact. They'd been waiting such a long time. Such a long time. They talked of their world, so different from ours. You see our Sun has just passed through an area of dark matter in the Milky Way galaxy,' said Johnson. 'As you know the world's particle accelerators can make tiny black holes. These tiny points of extreme gravity have become doors for the dark pressure to enter our universe. They hide in the shadows, travelling down dark matter tendrils and in the quiet of the mine they found me.'

'Why you?' asked Mel.

'They didn't say. The next day it happened again. This time it was for longer. But this time I saw them.'

'How could you 'see' anything in the dark? Did they give off light or something?' asked Mel.

'Not light,' continued Johnson. 'Their kind makes up so much of the mass of the universe. We are so small in comparison. So small they didn't even know about us until recently. They think of the Universe as theirs. This fifteen percent, that's all we are, our bodies, our homes, our planet, all the things we can see and touch are made of gravity-giving stuff comprising atoms made up of nuclei surrounded by electrons, which emit their electro-magnetic fields. But out there, in all that blackness, they lived. And now they're here,' said Johnson.

'That didn't answer my question,' said Olivia.

Johnson rambled on more and they had all had enough, even Jones. Outside, Mel thought Jones would be on his way. But as they made their way to their cars, Olivia revealed more about the day's plans than she had said thus far.

'I know, I know, he's coming with us to Boulby. Come on. Let's at least get there first,' said Mel.

Once in the car and on the road, they spoke about the events inside the hospital.

'I read somewhere about a boy that communicated with some other intelligence through the light of an old television set,' said Olivia. 'I wonder if it's a similar thing here, although a negative version, an inversion? What do you think?'

'I never heard that. I don't know what to think. Other than the poor man is ill,' said Mel.

'Let's take you down into the lab. See what you think there. Perhaps he did imagine the whole thing. Let's invoke Occam's Razor. The most simplest explanation is most probably the truth. It's a weird enough place. Perhaps it was just the stress of the job.'

For a site so large and deep it's odd that Boulby is so difficult to find. It's as if it does not want to be discovered. First there's the winding, sometimes icy coastal road heading north of Whitby; then the lengthy procedures involved in actually getting down there.

'It's not a job for you if you're claustrophobic,' said Olivia as they parked up and were soon met by Jones. 'I'm not, but I sympathise with that condition. The journey down, down, down, in that dark, cramped cage would be enough to finish you off.' She looked with disdain at Jones as she spoke, trying to illicit some reaction. 'We need to be at the deepest point where the new lab was built. It's 1,100 metres below the surface, over half a mile down below the moors.'

After a brief welcome from two male scientists, they were ushered into a changing room to put on orange overalls, big boots, hard hats with lamps and emergency breathing apparatus strapped to their belts.

'I often think about what would happen if anything went wrong,' Olivia continued as they entered a cage lift with a few others. They were all dressed the same so could be either physicists or miners, thought Mel.

'We'd be trapped down here beneath layers of water-filled rock at nearly twice the depth of that mine in Chile where those men had their narrow escape,' said Olivia.

'Yes, if something happened down here, we'd be stuck for a long, long time where the temperature can reach 40°C,' said one of their two guides, Doctor Barachiel. 'All that rock and water above stops the corrupting influence of cosmic rays and radiation that bombards the Earth's surface. Only the strangest particles make their way down here and that's what we're after.'

Air rushed past them as they descended in the cage lift, deeper and darker for seven long minutes. At the bottom of the pit were tunnels, lit with strip lights. They parted company with the others who had shared the lift. They were miners, and went off in the other direction towards the pit face, off to mine potash and alum as has been done here for over four hundred years in these caverns. The science party headed the other way, down a long, long tunnel, one of many in the immense honeycomb of over six hundred miles of passages. The tunnels were rough hewn from rock, tall and wide, wide enough for a Land Rover to drive past them. It was warm, but not uncomfortable with a taste of salt on the lips. The two women, Jones and the two other scientists who'd welcomed them at the top, got in another car and drove for half a mile to a small side tunnel. They stopped here for a coffee before entering the changing area and putting on new clean boots, hats and disposable white overalls.

'The lab must be kept as pristine as possible. We'll pass through what looks like a shower, but it's actually a vacuum that sucks up every last speck of dust,' said Doctor Dumah. Probably a South American accent, thought Mel.

Then at last they arrived in the laboratory itself, an unremarkable looking, one hundred metre long room with strip lights along the ceiling and weird purple walls. Overhead were rails for a heavy lifting crane and along one wall were banks of monitors, dials, wires and complex machinery. In the middle was a very large box, a cube with sides twenty metres across, covered in what looked like bubble-wrap.

'The search for dark matter is one of the aims of the six billion pounds Large Hadron Collider project at CERN in Switzerland, and a major goal of other American and European projects,' said the other man, Doctor Barachiel, 'This very British attempt is costing less than £1 million a year to run.'

'Have you found anything?' asked Jones.

'In the course of a six-month experiment run, we'd expect to detect no more than a handful of dark matter events,' said Dumah.

'Over the same period, we'll detect millions of background events, which come from traces of radioactivity in the detection equipment, in the laboratory walls, from those few cosmic rays that have managed to penetrate this deep underground,' joined in Barachiel.

'This is why the ZEPLIN-IV detector is swathed in protective material. The outer layer of polypropylene is designed to help eliminate neutrons; the thick lead casing around it is meant to eliminate gamma rays. Inside is the detector itself, the pure liquid xenon, which reacts every time one of its nuclei is hit by a particle,' said Dumah.

'Nothing very exciting happened for months on end. Until two days ago,' said Barachiel. 'The readings went crazy. There were events all over the place. We know that the salt in the atmosphere plays havoc with the electrical equipment, but nothing could have prepared us for this.'

'It was then that the power went off and Johnson had his 'episode',' said Barachiel.

Nothing remarkable happened in the mine on their visit. No events of any interesting particles were detected and even the project supervisor, Professor Khamael, could offer no explanation for either the massive burst of readings, or Johnson's reaction to it. The party returned to the surface. Jones was clearly relieved to be back above ground.

'I'll write my story, but it'll be a bit of a mystery without an explanation. Call me if you find anything out,' he handed Olivia and Mel a business card each.

Mel smiled and put it in her pocket. Olivia dropped hers in the cigarette bin outside the facility's door. The day had flown by quicker than they'd imagined and it was now getting dark. They'd had no lunch either so Olivia suggested fish and chips at Whitby on the way back.

They parked up on the cliff at Whitby and walked past the Captain Cook statue and down the steps to the pier. Mel could hear the roar of the waves crashing up the slipway. Looking west they saw the last of the Sun as it slipped into the sea and the strange pinkish light became purple and then black. They bought some fish and chips and walked out on the pier. Mel felt a sense of foreboding in the darkness. She thought about how in the dark the light you see is reduced to a few pin like sources, pricking out tiny details in the blackness. Perhaps Johnson was right, you can see the power of darkness, an unconquerable world of unknowable depths. She looked over the railings into the deep sea. The lights of the harbour and from the church up on the headland in front of the Abbey ruins seemed to wink like angels in the dark, cutting through the blackness like sharp pins through thick dark velvet.

In the hospital, Johnson was still at it.

'The Great Pyramid of Khufu was called, in ancient times, 'The Mountain of Light',' he rambled. 'It was coated in polished limestone and even during the time of Christ would have gleamed in the Sun. But that's not all. If you look at the schematics of the internal structure, the solid granite passageways built with solid sandstone blocks, with chambers and the vertical shaft that descends straight down into a deep underground well. Do you see? Don't you realise what it was? It was a dark matter converter!'

The nurse smiled, not that it could be seen in the dark of course.

Mel and Olivia returned to the car. Barney looked up, smelling the last of the fish.

'Hard luck,' said Olivia.

They drove off, back up across the moor to get home. It was one of those nights, with no Moon and just enough cloud cover to mean no stars, that feels so much darker than a usual night. They had just turned the corner onto the road at the top which would turn to drop down to Olivia's cottage, when the car seemed to lose power.

'What's the matter?' asked Mel.

'I don't know, I've got my foot flat on the pedal. It's not making any difference.'

The car got slower and slower.

Back in the darkened room, Johnson continued.

'Why do you think we have Diwali, the festival of light, Samhain, even Christmas lights?' he said. 'Christ said he was 'the light of the world', the light that was supposed to push back and banish the darkness. Not just so we can see and keep warm while the Sun is away during night and the winter, but so we are not taken by the creature that is the Dark.'

A different nurse came in.

'We need to get him to take the tablets. They're on the tray.'

The two nurses fumbled around in the dark as one took the tray from the other.

'Time for your tablets Mr Johnson,' said the nurse with the tray. She managed to put it down safely and pick up the pot of tablets and a glass of water.

'What did you think Hallowe'en is?' ranted Johnson. 'All Hallows Eve, the night that the veil is thinnest between this world and the other. So thin, so thin. Like now. It's never been so thin. We're always susceptible at this time of year. But now it's different. This time, they're here.'

The nurse approached the bed and felt around. Could Johnson have moved she thought? Was he walking around?.

'Where are you?' she asked.

'I'm here,' came Johnson's voice from behind her. It sounded different, lower.

'What, where?' she asked again.

'I'm here,' the voice said again.

The nurse paused, then walked towards the voice, bumping into the other nurse.

'Where are you Mr Johnson?' she said.

'I'm on top of nurse Janet,' said the grating voice.

Nurse Janet fell to the floor. The other nurse ran to the door and flicked a switch. The lights blinked on. As they did there was a eerie scream. Later, the nurse said it could have been Johnson, but she didn't believe it was. She looked around the room. Nurse Janet was getting to her feet. There was the bed, some side cupboards and a table. Johnson was not there. The nurse shivered. She had the feeling that he hadn't been there for a long, long time. Then the lights went out. The nurse recognised the next scream as her own.

'I'm going to pull over,' said Olivia as she turned off the road onto a verge. The engine stalled and fell silent. Olivia tried the key to start it up again but to no avail. Then the headlights began to dim. It was if the battery was being drained almost instantly. Barney whimpered. It was dark, very dark. Mel couldn't see her hand in front of her face. She got out of the car.

'Where are you?' Olivia called out to her.

Look!' shouted Mel looking up and ahead. There appeared to be three shimmering feint shapes, floating over the Moor, perhaps just a few yards in front, perhaps further away, coming towards them at walking pace. Each shape appeared to be about the height of a person.

'Can't you see?' said a voice, cracking up as if coming through an old radio. It may have been Johnson's voice. 'Sufficiently advanced life forms will not just be unrecognisable as life, but will blend so utterly completely into the fabric of what you call nature, that they will be nature. They have already experienced eight billion years of evolutionary time. Imagine a living state that manipulates luminous matter for their own purposes. They are the rightful owners of this Universe. They are the gods. They are space. They make time. Do you realise that? By expanding the Universe, they are gifting us time.'

Barney whimpered as the figures floated closer. Mel fiddled with her phone. There was no light from it. The silence was broken by the sound of a car coming their way. As the car approached its headlight could be seen, illuminating the road as it wound its way towards them. The car drove past, its headlights flooded the Triumph and the women in light. Then it zoomed past and was gone. So were the figures. Olivia's car's dashboard lights come back on. Olivia turned the ignition key and the car started again.

'Let's get back,' said Olivia. Mel nodded and got back in the car.

In the hospital the nurses were trying to explain what had

happened to the doctor. The lights were back on now. Johnson was not there. The last time anyone had seen him was of course not long after he had been brought in, now over twenty four hours earlier. Later on, Mel and Olivia spoke to the nurses and discussed their testimony. They then agreed to meet one last time with the reporter. This time in an Edwardian coffee shop in Whitby.

'So where did he go do you think?' asked Jones.

'You can't turn that much mass into energy in one go. Not in a traditional sense. Not with what we know about physics. It would release an explosion larger than the biggest atomic bomb,' said Olivia.

'But someone can't just disappear can they?' said Jones.

'I don't know,' said Mel, 'I'm thinking about what the nurses said, about there being an intelligence in the dark matter. We assume it's homogenous. But it could be as varied and rich as our own matter and energy. It could have its own versions of photons, electrons, protons and so on. Which is sort of what he was saying. Perhaps life has existed in this dark dimension for far longer than in our luminous one.'

'And now it wants to get in contact?' said Jones.

'Or maybe it's been in touch before,' said Olivia.

'What if there was a way, beyond our feeble attempts to detect dark matter, to somehow convert our luminous world into the fabric of the dark?' pondered Mel. 'Was that what happened? The dark was able to become corporeal through Johnson and those figures we saw.

What if it somehow converted him, uploaded him to the dark?'

'Are you thinking this dark universe is a sort of afterlife?' said Jones.

They became aware of the Christmas songs playing in the background in the cafe.

'Obviously not,' said Olivia.

'What if Jesus came from this dark dimension?' said Jones. 'Perhaps the 'Holy Spirit' that got Mary pregnant came from there. Perhaps the 'resurrection' was him being beamed back there, just like how Johnson disappeared?'

'Rubbish,' said Olivia.

'Well I think it's a story,' said Jones.

'What's a story?' said Olivia sarcastically.

'That the search for dark matter has found an intelligence living there. That it's been in contact with humans before. That it came and took Johnson and turned him into dark matter. And that the dark dimension may be really a spirit realm where we go when we die.'

'Good luck with that,' said Olivia.

'There was something he said. Something Johnson said about 'making time,' pondered Mel. 'Life absorbs energy such as visible light from the Sun, we call it low-entropy energy. Low entropy because it's ordered, not disordered. We do some useful work with it and transform it into lower grade, more chaotic higher-entropy energy as waste heat. Eventually all the energy will end up as background heat that we can't do anything with.'

'It's called heat death, yes. That would be the end of the Universe,' said Olivia.

'But luckily we live in an expanding and therefore constantly cooling Cosmos. As the Universe expands, it cools and creates more time. What if, and it's a big if, some hypothetical civilisation, eight billion years ago began to run out of fresh sources of energy and found a way to get the universe to cool even faster? One theory calls it 'quintessence', a relative of the Higgs field that permeates the cosmos. Perhaps some clever form of life, billions of years ago, figured out how to activate that field?'

'How?' said Jones.

'I have no idea. Maybe one day we'll find out,' said Mel.

The Christmas songs played as they walked out from The Rusty Shears courtyard into the night and they walked up the street to the west cliff where their cars were parked. Mel paused at the cliff edge to look over the pier, the dark black sea and sky, with the lights along the harbour, supplemented with twinkling Christmas lights, blinking away to puncture the blackness. Far out at sea, pinpoints of lights from ships slowly made their way across the North Sea. The clouds drifted away to reveal the myriad of stars of the Milky Way, glimmering down. All these tiny, tiny, lights, thought Mel, adrift in space, along with us, in the great Cosmic dark.

About the author

Ayd Instone is Head of Physics at Fyling Hall School. He runs a creative writing club *The Intergalactic Writers' Guild* to encourage students (aged 11 to 18) to write their own stories. This helps with both their English and Science studies. Ayd has a Masters in Teaching and Learning from the University of Oxford. Prior to teaching he was an international speaker on creativity and innovation, a singer/songwriter, graphic artist and an occasional comedian. He lives in Robin Hood's Bay with his wife, three children and two cats.

Sometimes he writes on his blog: http://aydinstone.wordpress.com/

You can see videos of Ayd performing on YouTube and at:

www.aydinstone.com

@aydinstone

Ayd Instone

SUNMAKERS
Publish your expertise

www.sunmakers.co.uk

Made in the USA
Columbia, SC
14 March 2018